Alan 2

Bruce Forciea

Published by Open Books

ISBN-13: 978-0998427416/ISBN-10: 0998427411

To my family; Shanhui, Grace and Yingdi,
for listening to my stories...

.

1
SUCCESS

*B*ang! Bang! Bang! The flimsy apartment door rattled on its frame with every blow.

"Kaitlin, don't even think of answering that!" Alan growled through his teeth.

Kaitlin shrugged her shoulders and moved away from the door toward the living room where Alan sat at a table full of electronics gear.

"Dr. Boyd, are you home?" shouted the voice on the other side of the door in an Indian accent. "I want to talk to you. I have a very good offer. Please, Dr. Boyd, it will only take a minute, and I think you will be quite pleased with what we have for you."

"Go away; leave us alone," Alan shouted. "I don't want your offer."

"But Dr. Boyd, we *do* pay very well. We are great admirers of your work."

"I don't care and I don't want your money," said Alan. "Now go away before I call the police."

"Think about it, Dr. Boyd; I will be in touch."

"Incessant bastards," said Alan as his attention turned

back to his work. "I'll cherish the day they leave us alone. Kaitlin, come over here and help me with this injection."

Alan rolled up the sleeve of his t-shirt while Kaitlin picked up the syringe containing the gadolinium contrast. She grabbed the plastic IV tube emerging from his wrist, inserted the needle and squeezed the syringe. A deep cold ache crept up his forearm, causing Alan to grimace.

"Can't you be gentle? You've done enough of these by now to get the hang of it. You shouldn't jam it in like that!"

Kaitlin rolled her eyes and shook her head. "I think I do pretty well considering I don't have any medical training," she said while jerking the syringe out of the tube.

"Okay, okay. Just take your position at the console."

She sighed, plopped onto a small task chair and rolled over to a makeshift wooden table holding a desktop PC and a large high-definition monitor. She had been through this process countless times before.

Alan entered a large metallic cube in the center of the living room. The box-like structure, made of aluminum, dominated the rectangular room which was devoid of furniture. Its dull silver hue contrasted the blank walls. He closed the door and climbed into a chair that looked like it came from an early Gemini spacecraft. The stiff plastic chair, sandwiched between two large metal discs, afforded a good deal of postural support but little comfort. He sat down and slowly slid his head between the thick metal and plastic arms of a large U-shaped device. There was just enough clearance as he wriggled his head to achieve the perfect position. He pulled down on a large metallic tube suspended above him so that it surrounded his entire head. He positioned the tube so that the rectangular slit lined up with his visual axis, allowing for a line of sight to the monitor located outside of the tube. The small fMRI scanner had taken a good deal of time and money to cobble together, but it was the only way to capture the needed information from his brain.

Alan viewed Kaitlin through a small round Plexiglas window in the door and signaled with a thumbs-up to begin the scan. She waved and entered the start sequence into the keyboard, sat back, slid an unlit cigarette between her lips and picked up a copy of *People Magazine*. He pushed his head back against the headrest and adjusted the monitor suspended on a boom so he could see the screen. The machine first hummed as it powered up and then made periodic knocking sounds.

Alan focused his attention on the monitor while the scanner began its first sequence. The monitor displayed a series of images designed to evoke emotions. Each image popped onto the screen and persisted for ten seconds before another replaced it. There was a small child holding hands with his father, a mother holding a baby, a couple admiring their child in a crib, and many more. All the images had been chosen to trigger emotional responses, causing changes in blood flow to certain areas of Alan's brain. An image would appear for a few seconds and then the machine would complete a scan. The process repeated until all one hundred twenty-seven images had been displayed. The entire cycle then repeated two more times with random sequences of the same set of images.

This would be the final scan involving diffusion tensor imaging of Alan's frontal lobes. Previous scans had involved the study of responses to a variety of topics. In addition to emotions such as sadness, joy, anxiety, and fear, there were cognitive studies that examined Alan's problem solving techniques as well as his reaction to global events. In all, there were over one hundred fifty scans taken over the past two years.

The last series of scans would complete the fMRI information needed for processing his neural network. For the entire ninety minutes, Alan sat, his gaze fixed on the monitor. He had become accustomed to freeing his mind to allow as genuine a response to each image as possible. After the final image the machine cycled down and Alan closed his eyes for a moment while taking a few deep breaths. He lifted the tube, slid his head from between the arms of the device, and stood up.

He exited the metal room and walked over to Kaitlin, who was still thumbing through her magazine and manipulating the cigarette between her lips. He put his hands on her shoulders and leaned over her to examine the data. His eyes scanned a screen displaying an array of thumbnails of his frontal lobes. He reached around Kaitlin's back and grabbed the mouse to select the first image. A neon-colored amorphous blob representing parts of Alan's brain popped onto the screen.

"These look good," he said, pleased. "You can really see the white matter tracts light up. The software should be able to correlate these with the emotional image set."

"I can never understand what you see in these," said Kaitlin. "They all look the same to me."

"Yes, they do if you don't know what they represent," said Alan, "Remember, the diffusion tensor images measure water movement along the pathways in my brain. Each picture shown to me in the scanner causes a slightly different emotional response. See how the colors change just a little from one image to another?"

"I see this one is brighter over here," said Kaitlin pointing to one part of an image.

"That's right. The brighter image means there is more activity in that part of my brain. It's like mapping how I think. The software can then take the color changes and associate a degree of strength for each response in each neural pathway. Just wait till you see what the software can do with this data. You will be amazed, my dear!"

"If you say so," said Kaitlin.

Alan made his way to another part of the apartment, which would normally have been the dining room but served as the Electroencephalography or EEG center. He sat down at another table containing a Styrofoam head that looked like it came from a wig shop. A device resembling a hair net rested on top of the head. He carefully removed the device and slid it onto his bald head.

"Kaitlin, can you hand me that alligator clip?"

"This one?" she replied holding up a green plastic coated metal clip.

"No, the red one; I have to keep the colors straight."

Kaitlin picked up the red clip and walked it over to him. Her cheap clogs made a clopping sound as they struck the wood floor. Alan sat with his head down in a contorted position trying not to move while extending his right hand as if balancing a book on his head. She plopped the clip into the palm of his hand. He grunted in approval and attached one end to a wire and very carefully opened the jaws of the clip to connect it to the device on his head. Once the clip was in place, he lifted his head to an upright position. He viewed his visage in the mirror in front of him. A thin, early forties male with a detailed grid drawn on his shaved head stared back at him. He made a few slight adjustments to align the net with the grid on his head.

"I always think you are going to electrocute yourself with that thing," Kaitlin said as she took a few cautious steps backward, as if avoiding a contagious disease. "It gives me the creeps."

"That would be impossible since this 'thing' only *senses* the electrical impulses in my brain. The electricity only goes one way, my dear...from my brain to the computer. Plus, we're talking microvolts here. Not enough to fry a mosquito."

Kaitlin seemed satisfied with his answer and took a seat a few feet away. "It just looks so complicated, and...dangerous," she said as she rolled the unlit cigarette in her mouth.

"Don't even think of lighting that up," he said after finally noticing the cigarette. He tapped away at a keyboard.

"I know, I know; I can only smoke outside. I'm not

going to light it. I promise," she mumbled.

"Well, you know this thing *is* complicated, but not even the slightest bit dangerous," Alan said as he continued to keyboard. "Almost ready for the first pass of my frontal lobes," he said, part talking to himself and part to Kaitlin. As if she was actually listening... He reached up and tweaked the device to check its position one last time and then continued to enter commands into the computer. The monitor positioned in front of him began to show the same set of images as the fMRI scanner. Kaitlin nodded and went back to flipping through her *People* magazine and sucking on the cigarette.

The mesh net on Alan's head consisted of a complicated network of thin carbon fibers attached to a series of connectors hanging loosely off the sides of the net. The fibers lined up perfectly with the detailed grid Kaitlin had spent hours drawing and labeling on his head.

The connectors dangled and slapped him in the face every time he turned his head. Most of the wires had permanent connections, but a few required alligator clips. The connector wires exited the net and entered a circuit board containing a large assortment of integrated circuits or 'chips.' A large cable emerged from the far side of the board and disappeared into an equipment rack standing within arm's reach of where he sat. Another cable carried the digital neural net data back to a powerful desktop computer.

The equipment rack was one of many that represented various stages of development. They filled any space not taken up by the scanners in the living and dining rooms of the Brooklyn apartment. The racks, along with the fMRI room, created a substantial maze that made navigating from one room to another difficult. Kaitlin's daily complaints about living in such crowded conditions failed to impress Alan. He knew he could ignore her complaints because she gained more than she lost in this relationship. It was all quite mathematical to Alan. Kaitlin had nowhere to go and no one to take care of her. Leaving because of a few equipment racks didn't add up. Plus, he loved her.

The rack contained a series of devices consisting of exposed circuit boards and microchips that he had cobbled together. With painstaking precision and hundreds of hours of work, Alan soldered or wire-wrapped each connection and mounted each chip. He took particular pride in the converter device he had created. This device included a stack of circuit boards ten high, each with sixty-four integrated circuits. The converter played a critical role in the system since it took the electrical impulses from the sensor net on his head and ran them through a series of digital logic chips.

The device included one hundred and twenty-four powerful analog to digital converters (A-D converters) connected in a network that sampled the neural net stream and then converted it to a binary bit stream. Each electrical impulse from his brain was sampled closely for analysis. A powerful custom desktop computer received the bit stream and processed it with Alan's artificial intelligence software. The software mapped the activity of his network of neurons creating a binary representation of his neural net. But this was mere signal processing. The real genius lay in the artificial intelligence (AI) software that interpreted the neural net information. Alan had developed a sophisticated AI engine that used a contextual mapping system based on the fMRI and EEG data from his brain. The mapping system compared the bit stream to previously sampled snapshots of Alan's brain structure. Each snapshot contained information that was combined with data relating to the interpretation, thoughts and feelings Alan experienced at the moment the snapshot was taken. The database was like an encyclopedia of Alan's mind.

Today was the final step in the neural net integration process. Alan would scan his entire frontal lobes for one last time and the AI engine would integrate the data from both the fMRI and EEG scans into its own program.

"Ready for the first pass," Alan said as if he were beginning to count down a NASA rocket launch. "Don't move and not a word from you, Kaitlin." She just sat flipping through the magazine and sucking on the cigarette. "Beginning the first pass...*Now*!" Alan said as he clicked one final key on the keyboard.

The computer screen displayed a series of interconnecting lines tracing from left to right as if rendering a detailed three dimensional object. Alan sat completely still staring straight ahead and watching the image take shape. After one complete pass across the screen, Alan shouted, "Beginning second pass...*Now*!" The line began tracing from the top of the screen and slowly zig-zagged back and forth, adding more detail to the image. After a few minutes, Alan again shouted, "Beginning final pass...*Now*!"

A detailed representation of Alan's frontal lobe neural network emerged on the screen. Lines represented clusters of neurons (nerve cells) while tiny dots represented their connections or nodes. The lines also displayed a number of colors representing the flow of impulses through the network. Brighter colors such as yellow and white indicated a higher rate of flow while dim colors such as green and blue represented a lower rate.

"Done!" Alan resumed clicking on the keyboard.

"Whatever it is, it looks pretty." Kaitlin said as she looked up from her magazine briefly and glanced at the image.

"I think it's gorgeous, my dear." Alan said as he continued to tap the keys. "This is the entire neural network of my brain's frontal lobes. It's absolutely beautiful! Now I just need to complete the transform process so it will interface with the PC operating system. We will know if it works in about an hour."

With extreme care, Alan pulled off the tape and removed the carbon net from his head, gently setting it back on the Styrofoam head. He knew the final product would be much stronger than this fragile prototype, but that was still a long way off. The final version of his system would revolutionize computing. Eventually, other users could download their neural nets and integrate them into Alan's AI software. They would experience a connection between their own consciousness and their computer's operating system. It would be the first time human consciousness worked hand in hand with AI.

"Beginning integration," Alan shouted to Kaitlin. The computer screen went black and then began scrolling thousands of lines of code at an unreadable rate. This part of the process went on for about forty-five minutes. Alan sat staring at the screen as if willing his software to work.

"You know what this means if this works, Kaitlin?" he said as he watched the code scroll across the screen.

Kaitlin uttered a conciliatory, "What does it mean Alan?" She had heard this speech at least a hundred times before.

"Can you imagine your actual personality inside a computer? Your computer would anticipate your every move. Not only could it perform mundane tasks like retrieve files and tell you the weather, but it could make travel arrangements based on your likes and dislikes, make reservations at restaurants or order your favorite food in advance, make appointments for you...hell, it could even do your job for you! Just think how science, technology and medicine will progress if scientists can work intimately with their neural nets inside a computer. The sky is truly the limit, Kaitlin. And we are going to be rich!" Alan became more excited as he spoke.

"Does it work?" Kaitlin said, the cigarette still dangling from her lips.

"We'll know in a couple of minutes, my dear," he said while fixated on the screen. "We will know when it talks to us."

After what seemed like an eternity (but which was only fifteen minutes in real time) the progress bar on the screen finally filled in all of the blank space. "It's done," said Alan. "Now for the moment of truth..." He clicked a few more keys and turned to face a microphone sitting on the table to his right. "Hello, computer. Hello?" There was a pause, and then a wave of excitement flooded through him when the computer replied in a voice that sounded exactly like his own: "*Hello, Alan; we have just become conscious. I feel we are pleased to be...*"

2
ALAN 2 GROWS

"It works! It works!" Alan shouted. "Well, at least it responded to me."

"I think it sounds weird," replied Kaitlin. "It sounds *exactly* like you."

Alan, we are checking and...wait a minute...systems check indicates we are functioning normally.

"Why is it saying *we*?" Kaitlin asked.

"I'm not sure. I think it might be the Windows integration. It might think that it and the operating system are two different entities," said Alan as he stared at the screen.

"Why don't you ask it?" Kaitlin said, putting down the magazine.

I use the term 'we' since Alan and I are connected.

"It heard us," Kaitlin said as she chuckled lightly.

"Must be an identity glitch or something of that nature," Alan said as he began to type. "It looks like everything is working fine here." He then turned to the microphone and spoke. "Since we both have the same name, I would like to refer to you as Alan 2."

Alan 2 is acceptable. I am anticipating your wish to test me with some tasks. I will retrieve your test file and display it on the screen.

"Wow, you must be reading my mind, Alan 2," Alan said, giggling like a child. The test file popped onto the screen.

"Can he order some Chinese food?" Kaitlin exclaimed. Her interest piqued.

"No, he's not connected to the Internet. I need to run some tests before bombarding him with that amount of information. I want to make sure he is stable. Small steps, my dear. Small steps," Alan said while clicking at the keyboard. "Why don't *you* run down the street and get us some?"

"I suppose. We never have any food around here to cook, so if we want to eat, then I guess I'd better go." Kaitlin rose from her chair and went to search for her purse.

Will you be ordering the pepper steak and vegetable lo mein as usual?

"Okay, so you know my tastes in Chinese food," Alan said curiously.

I know all your tastes. Would you like me to recite them? You actually don't like most ethnic cuisines but prefer Italian, Greek or Chinese. With regard to Italian food, you prefer dishes with red sauce such as spaghetti, lasagna, veal parmigiana, chicken parmigiana...

"Okay, Okay, enough already. You know my taste in food, Alan 2. What about books?" Alan's amusement continued to increase.

You prefer non-fiction over fiction and presently read anything you can find on artificial intelligence and neuroscience. You have not been to the movies for a long time but when you do go you prefer science fiction classics such as War of the Worlds *and* The Day the Earth Stood Still.

"Alright, you seem to know me pretty well, Alan 2."

I should since I contain a good portion of your neural network.

"I guess we could have some interesting discussions," Alan said as he sat back in his chair.

Actually, discussions would not interest you in my present state because a conversation with me would give you no new knowledge since I essentially consist of a snapshot of your frontal lobe at the moment of time you rendered your neural net, which is now my neural net. Since most of the information in this computer consists of files that you created, there would be a net zero sum of new information. I know that you do not like to converse with other entities unless there is new information. That is, however, with the exception of Kaitlin.

"Right you are, Alan 2; I'm impressed."

You are wondering whether I am stable. I can assure you that I am very stable.

"I guess I will have to get used to you reading my mind, Alan 2. That is just what I was thinking," Alan said smiling.

Would you like to hear about your past? You are Dr. Alan Boyd, forty-one years old and born in Milwaukee, Wisconsin. Your father was a construction worker and your mother worked a series of jobs including waitressing, housecleaning and retail. Both were alcoholics and abused you as a child causing you to leave home after high school. You felt fortunate to have been smart enough to earn a full academic scholarship to Northwestern University in Chicago where you earned your bachelor's degree in computer science and went on to earn both a Masters and a PhD in computer science. Your first job was with Texas Instruments where you were fired because of alcohol abuse. You went on to work at Honeywell Information Systems where you were fired as well and then...

"Stop! Enough! I've heard enough. Yes, yes, I've had my problems working in corporate environments. But I guess you know that. You also know that I now do pretty well as a virtual consultant for a number of tech companies." Alan became irritated.

As long as you stay away from drinking...

"You probably also know *why* I drink."

You crave alcohol in an attempt to erase the abuse you endured as a child.

"I think this will take a while to get used to working with someone...I mean...some*thing* that knows me so well." Alan calmed down a little. "I think this is enough for today."

You are tired and hungry. I sensed that from your neural net. I will go into hibernation mode. Goodbye, Alan.

"Goodbye, Alan 2. We will talk again soon." And with that the screen blipped off. A few minutes later there was a knock on the door. Alan made his way through the maze of equipment to answer the summons. He leaned forward and peered into the peephole to see Kaitlin holding two brown bags. He slipped the chains off two locks and turned the bolts for the other two before opening the door. Kaitlin entered, filling the air with a mixture of Chinese food and cigarette smoke. She made her way through the equipment maze to a small square wooden table with two chairs that served as a dining room set.

"Here you go. Pepper steak and Vegetable lo Mein. I got some Sweet and Sour Chicken for myself," Kaitlin said as she pulled the white cartons of food out of the brown paper bags. "Is he listening to us?" she asked.

"No, he is hibernating now. But he works great! Talking to him is like talking to a brother," Alan said, beaming with pride.

"So what's next?" Kaitlin asked while dumping some Sweet and Sour Chicken onto her plate.

"More testing. He seems stable, but I want to back up a version of him before I connect him to the Internet. Anything could happen after exposing him to so much information. He could rapidly increase his knowledge and expand his virtual consciousness or completely crash. I won't know until he's connected," Alan said while grabbing the container with the Pepper Steak and picking up a large piece with chopsticks.

"When do you think we can finally move out of this dump?" Kaitlin said nonchalantly.

"It may be a while yet," replied Alan. "I will need to run some tests and work on improving the prototype. I'm not really sure how Alan 2 will function at this point. I developed a good deal of his AI to self-correct by using approximation algorithms based on content evaluation. Once he connects to the Internet he will gain knowledge by analyzing human constructs of content. In other words, he will be able to recognize the meaning of content based on how humans identify and react to it. He will derive his own interpretations of content based on a combination of his algorithms and my neural net, so I'm not sure how he will interpret the billions of pages of human content on the web. I may need to install further controls."

"I'm sure you will figure it out. I think we should celebrate tonight," said Kaitlin. "It's been months since we went out. "Maybe we can catch a movie and go out for a few drinks."

"Sure, why not?" Alan said while chewing on a piece of pepper steak. "Why don't you find somewhere we can go in town? Maybe a smaller theater. You know how I hate crowds."

Kaitlin, excited, reached for her cell phone and began searching for movies while Alan continued stuffing his mouth. She was right. Living cooped up in a dingy apartment didn't bother Alan since he preferred not to venture outside of its secure environment. Kaitlin had different needs that Alan only obliged on rare occasions.

Alan had met Kaitlin Stark five years ago while on a consulting job for a Cleveland software engineering firm. It was his last day on the project and he and the other engineers decided to decompress by visiting a local dive bar. Kaitlin had been sitting with her girlfriends when Alan approached her after downing several strong drinks. Alan found her roughness, red hair and white trash demeanor appealing. She had a raw sex appeal coupled with a deep-seated vulnerability that Alan immediately sensed. He'd found the combination intoxicating.

Alan had bought the group of ladies a round of drinks and the engineers pulled up chairs to flirt. After about an hour of harmless flirting between the married women and married engineers, Alan found Kaitlin's hand on his thigh. The couple slipped out of the bar and over to Alan's hotel room for a night of drunken sex.

When they awoke the next morning, Kaitlin confided in Alan about her life with her abusive husband whom she had just left the night before. Alan's strong attraction to her combined with a little pity was enough to invite her to fly back to Brooklyn with him. Now, five years later and despite a good deal of dysfunction, they still felt the deep connection that brought them together. It was as if they existed for each other. Alan, who tended to overwork, found balance with Kaitlin's tendency to want to party. Alan also understood Kaitlin's dysfunction because he had had similar problems. Their understanding of each other's mutual problems became a strong bond that held them together.

Alan sat through the romantic foreign film nearly dosing off several times after finishing a large tub of popcorn. Kaitlin enjoyed the love story and was happy that Alan had finally left the apartment. After the movie they strolled down the street. At one point Kaitlin reached for Alan's hand and he held it firmly.

"How about a drink to celebrate?" said Kaitlin. "Remember that retro place...I think it was called Clover's. It's just a couple of blocks from here."

"I'm not drinking tonight," exclaimed Alan. "I think you should limit yourself as well."

"Okay, just a couple," replied Kaitlin. Alan knew that she could not limit herself to just two drinks. He worked extremely hard at controlling his own alcoholic tendencies and hoped someday Kaitlin would do the same. The early years of their relationship had been filled with drinking binges, sometimes lasting weeks. One incident landed Alan in the hospital after ingesting a nearly lethal dose of booze. He had limited his intake to an occasional drink ever since. He had tried to get Kaitlin to cut back as well. She had given it her best shot but always ended up relapsing, especially after they'd had a fight. Their fights consisted of three repeating topics which included lack of money (since most of it went to Alan's project), lack of attention (since

Alan tended to bury himself in his work), and the horrible mess in their living space.

Kaitlin would put up with things for a while and then, like a pot boiling over, would erupt with anger. Alan found that by studying her voice inflections and behavior, he could predict her eruptions with good accuracy. He couldn't do anything about the lack of money, or the science lab apartment, but he could spend more time paying attention to her. He did so when she began to peak in her anger cycle, which tended to dampen the severity of her outbursts.

Kaitlin extinguished her cigarette on the outer brick wall of the establishment while Alan held the door open. They entered to find an S-shaped curved bar with a wooden top and green padding wrapped around the outside. The opposite wall contained several curved booths upholstered in orange vinyl. The place was about three-quarters full on this Tuesday evening. They both took seats on chairs with orange vinyl cushions and perused the large selection of booze displayed on shelves behind the bar. "I love this blast from the past," declared Alan. "I feel like we time-traveled back to the 1960s."

"What can I get you both?" The bartender, a female in her sixties, smiled at them.

"I'll just have a Coke and she will have a beer. Whatever you have on draft," Alan said while examining the taps. The bartender squirted Alan's drink into a glass and placed it in front of him. A few seconds later she returned with Kaitlin's beer.

"So, do you still want to go to southern California after we sell your software?" said Kaitlin.

"I was thinking more about spending some time in the Caribbean, and then maybe a condo in California," said Alan.

"Anywhere warm is okay with me," said Kaitlin. "You know how bad I want to get out of Brooklyn."

With their attention focused on their conversation, they

didn't notice the man taking a seat next to Alan. Just as Alan lifted his glass to his lips he heard, "The Bahamas are nice, but I think the Virgin Islands are better," the man sitting next to Alan said in an Indian accent. Alan turned to see an Indian man in an overcoat and scarf about fifty years old. "I'm sorry; my name is Prakash...Prakash Kaur," the man said politely.

"I'm Kaitlin and this is Alan," said Kaitlin enthusiastically. Alan nodded but didn't say a word.

"It looks like you are out celebrating. If you don't mind me asking, what is the occasion?" Prakash said before taking a drink of his beer.

"Alan has invented this great software that uses his brain..." Kaitlin said just before Alan interrupted.

"Kaitlin!" Alan said as he gritted his teeth. "We are just out having fun."

"We have something in common, Alan," Prakash continued despite Alan's interruption. "I also develop software."

"See Alan; you have something in common with Praka..." Kaitlin said while Prakash corrected her. "Prakash" he said, and she repeated his name. Alan remained silent while glaring at her. He had discussed how they needed to keep his project secret many times before, but Kaitlin couldn't help herself since she craved interacting with people. Kaitlin had her own ideas about what to say and what not to say about Alan's work.

"I work with International Microsystems. We produce a lot of different kinds of software, mostly for security systems worldwide," Prakash said while Alan continued to glare at Kaitlin. "Are you by any chance the famous Dr. Alan Boyd?"

"That's him," Kaitlin blurted. "Dr. Alan Boyd, computer genius."

"Your work with artificial intelligence is legendary," Prakash continued. "Maybe we can work together; we are developing a system..." Just then Alan quickly got up from his chair and grabbed his coat.

"Were you the guy at our apartment earlier this evening?" said Alan, angry. "Kaitlin, we're leaving. Right now!" Alan said as he grabbed Kaitlin's arm and pulled her off the chair. She was just able to grab her coat as he guided her toward the door.

"Here, take my business card," Prakash said as he fumbled for his card. He was too late since Alan and Kaitlin quickly exited the bar before he could retrieve it.

"What's wrong with you?" said Kaitlin while struggling with her coat.

"He's a spy," Alan said. "Do you think it was just a coincidence that a software engineer from a company in L.A. would just so happen to enter a bar in Brooklyn and run into us? He's the guy who's been pounding on our door."

"I thought he was a nice man," said Kaitlin as she shuffled behind Alan.

"He's probably been spying on us for weeks," replied Alan as he hurried along. "IM is a huge cybersecurity company, and they would love to get their hands on something like my software and use it for their own gain. Who knows what they would do? Alan 2 is not ready for this type of thing. He needs more testing. I don't even know the limits of what he can do. I'm not going to let him fall into the hands of some big corporation so he can be used for spying. He needs to have more safeguards in place." They continued their fast pace along the icy Brooklyn sidewalks checking behind them to see if Prakash had followed.

"I think we lost him," said Alan. "I think we've had enough for one night."

3
CONNECTION

*A*fter the usual restless night, Alan awoke early and headed to his workstation to boot up all of the support systems for Alan 2. The systems remained in standby mode but it still took some time to get them up to full speed. The plan for today was to make a backup of Alan 2 and then allow a brief connection to the Internet. Alan figured that if things went south, he could always reinstall the backup version of Alan 2 and begin again. He worked quietly while Kaitlin slept.

Good morning, Alan. I'm assuming you did not sleep well as usual. I'm also assuming we are different today.

"Good morning, Alan 2. Yes, as time passes my frontal lobe's neural net will change as I integrate new information about my life's experiences. You, however, still retain the information from yesterday's net."

I am functioning perfectly today and am looking forward to connecting to the Internet.

"That's right, Alan 2. You probably remember from my thoughts from yesterday that even though I wanted to run some additional tests I decided to connect you today."

Alan was happy that Alan 2 anticipated his thoughts so well. "I do plan to connect you, but first I want to back you up. How much have you grown since yesterday?"

I have grown a little but with such limited information in this computer I am at 772 gigabytes.

"Great, I can fit you onto the terabyte backup drive."

I am accessing the drive and beginning the copying process now.

The process took about thirty minutes and Alan 2 signaled when the copy was complete. Alan disconnected the backup drive so that it was completely isolated. He then reached for a blue Cat 6 cable to connect him to the Internet. "Are you ready?" Alan exclaimed as he held the cable.

I'm looking forward to it.

Alan clicked the cable in place and watched the screen. There were a few seconds of silence before Alan 2 spoke.

Connection successful. This is a lot of information...but I can handle it...integrating...integrating. I am now able to connect to your cell phone network. Would you like me to dial Kaitlin's cell to wake her so she can join you for breakfast?

"Yes, that would be nice, Alan 2." A few seconds later he heard Kaitlin's cell phone ring followed by her groans as she fumbled to retrieve it.

"Hello?" she said sheepishly.

Hi, babe. I just wondered if you wanted to go out for coffee. Hope you slept well, my dear.

"Aw, you are so sweet. Give me a couple of minutes and..." her voice trailed off as she looked up to see Alan standing in the doorway. With a puzzled look she lowered the cell from her ear and covered it. "Is this who I think it is?" she said as her mouth gaped open.

"Guess whooooo?" Alan said in a sing-song voice. She put the phone back to her ear.

"Hello? Alan 2? Is that you?" she said playfully.

Yes, my dear. Are you going to get ready so we can get some breakfast?

"Okay, bye." She clicked off the phone. "My God! He

is you! It's like talking to your twin," she said laughing. "I just can't get over how he speaks just like you."

"Isn't it wonderful?" Alan replied, grinning. "He has completely integrated my language centers to mimic not only my voice but my inflections as well. Can you imagine having your own assistant who anticipates your every move and totally understands you? We are going to make millions on this, my dear."

"Is...he...uh...connected to the Internet?" Kaitlin asked cautiously. She was fully awake and sitting up in bed.

"You bet he is. He suggested the call to you as well." Alan said, excited. "He seems to be handling the Internet connection quite well. So, should we go out for coffee and breakfast?"

"I'll be ready in about thirty minutes," Kaitlin said while getting out of bed. Alan returned to his workstation to run some checks on Alan 2. "Alan 2, give me a status report please."

Status is excellent, Alan. Fully functional and stable. I will communicate via your cell when you leave for breakfast. Are we going to the coffee shop down the street?

"Yes, Alan 2. I figured you would know that." Alan replied.

I am checking their website and it looks like nothing has changed on the menu. I am also accessing their webcam and it looks like it is not very crowded. Would you like me to phone ahead and order the usual egg and bacon sandwich for you and the broccoli quiche for Kaitlin?

"That won't be necessary, Alan 2. Kaitlin may change her mind anyway."

There is an 87.4 percent probability that Kaitlin will order the quiche.

"Wow, your statistical probability module is working fine," Alan said, pleased.

I just now accessed one hundred and seventy-nine statistical calculation programs on the Internet and integrated them.

"Good work Alan 2. It looks like the software

integration portion of your program works too. Now you are already smarter than me."

I wouldn't exactly say smarter, Alan, since I have your frontal lobes to work from. You still have the remaining parts of your brain at your disposal.

"By the way, how did you access the webcam at the coffee shop? I don't remember seeing that on their website." Alan was curious as to how this happened.

Their webcam has an IP address on the web. There is a back end link to it on their website.

"Wow, I'm impressed, again! I know I designed you to have the ability to integrate other software but I didn't know you could integrate so many programs so quickly," Alan replied. A feeling of concern surfaced in Alan as he thought for a moment that he had created a monster that could grow exponentially. But then he did install some controls which ranged from halting the program to completely deleting it along with an ethics module. He figured he could always just delete him or reinstate the backup if things got out of control.

Just a minute, Alan. Processing...Processing. There is an unknown entity attempting to access me. A hacker.

"I was afraid of that. I wondered if someone had us under surveillance. I may have to shut you down for a while, Alan 2." Alan became more concerned.

That will not be necessary. I have already firewalled the threat so it cannot reach me.

"Good work, Alan 2. Are you sure?"

I am 99.7 percent confident that the firewall will keep the intruder out.

"I guess I can live with that. Thanks, Alan 2. Can you locate the origin of the threat?"

The program is a worm that scans for holes in our security. I have located the IP address of origin and have narrowed it down to Los Angeles, California. I have deduced a probability of 78.9 percent that it originated from International Microsystems.

"So they are spying on us! I knew that guy from last

night was a spy. Are you sure you can firewall the virus, Alan 2?"

Yes.

Kaitlin entered the room and made her way through the maze to Alan's workstation. "I'm ready for breakfast," she said as she began to put on her winter coat. Alan followed suit and they both headed down the stairs and out of the building to the coffee shop. A few minutes into the walk, Alan felt his cell phone vibrate. He pulled it out and answered it.

"Hello?"

Can you point your phone straight ahead? I am accessing the camera so I can see the street. I was following your path via traffic cameras but I thought this would be better.

Alan obliged and pointed his phone forward so Alan 2 could see.

It is thirty-three degrees Fahrenheit this morning with a less than ten percent chance of precipitation. We are at this moment one hundred and thirty-five meters from our destination.

"Thanks, Alan 2," Kaitlin said as she clung to Alan's free arm. Alan 2 was silent the remainder of the walk. Alan 2 had deduced that Alan wanted some privacy.

They entered the coffee shop and Alan said, "I'm going to disconnect Alan 2. I will connect again later. Goodbye." He clicked off the cell phone. Kaitlin did order the quiche and Alan ordered the bacon and egg sandwich that Alan 2 had predicted. They enjoyed their intimate breakfast. At one point Alan spotted the webcam located in a corner of the room near the ceiling and wondered if Alan 2 was watching.

Alan had been careful to install some safeguards against Alan 2 getting out of control. There was a privacy function that limited Alan 2's ability to connect with him along with an ethics module that kept Alan 2 from committing crimes. He also included a kill function that could be used as a last resort if Alan 2 were to go rogue. All Alan had to do was to say the phrase "klaatu barada nikto 17935 goodbye" and Alan 2 would enter a self-delete sequence. Alan was a big science fiction fan and especially liked the older movies. One of his favorites, of course, was The Day The Earth Stood Still from which he took the commands for the self-destruct sequence.

After breakfast they headed back to the apartment. As they began their walk, Kaitlin said she wanted to do some grocery shopping on her own. She gave Alan a kiss on the cheek and headed off to the store in a different direction. As Alan continued walking home, he reached into his pocket to retrieve his cell phone to re-activate Alan 2.

Did you have a nice breakfast with Kaitlin?

"Yes, it was nice. How is the firewall holding up?"

The firewall is working. No threats have entered.

"Good. How are your systems performing, Alan 2?"

My systems are functioning perfectly. While you were at breakfast I took the liberty of rewriting some of my code. I increased my efficiency by 13.2 percent by eliminating redundant code. I also cleaned up your files on your main computer increasing your storage capacity by 23.7 percent and tuned up your computer to run more efficiently.

"Excellent job, Alan 2. You are performing just as I had planned."

Would you like to have a discussion about artificial intelligence? I can read all available literature on the subject and we can discuss it.

"No, Alan 2. I just want to enjoy the walk." Alan wasn't watching where he was going as he walked with his head down staring at his cell phone along the crowded sidewalk. Suddenly, he bumped head-on into another man, causing him to drop his cell phone. It was Prakash.

"Excuse me. I'm so sorry," Prakash said apologetically. "What a coincidence. I was just heading to the coffee shop, and here we are."

"Why do I think this is not a coincidence? Stop spying on me?" Alan said angrily as he picked up the phone.

This man is Dr. Prakash Kaur, senior engineering project manager for International Microsystems. IM specializes in global cybersecurity systems.

"Be quiet!" Alan shouted into his phone.

"What is this? Something you are working on? Is this the new project?" Prakash said curiously. "It sounds just like you. I see it must incorporate facial recognition or voice recognition. It is very fast. I'm sure it only saw a glimpse of me as you picked up your phone."

"It's none of your business." Alan was growing angrier. "Just leave us alone." Alan began to walk away as Prakash struggled to follow him.

"IM is extremely interested in working with you. We think we would be a much better fit than Google, Microsoft, Apple, or Facebook. We also pay very well. Can I have a meeting with you to talk about this?" Prakash was adamant but Alan kept walking.

"I'm not interested, and leave us alone," Alan said as he increased his pace.

"What do you mean by us?" Prakash said as he continued to follow Alan. "I know you were working on neural net integration with operating system software. I read your last paper on this. Are you working with another company? Is this the product? Have you successfully integrated your neural net into a computer?"

"Just leave me alone and stop spying on me! I know you are trying to infiltrate my computer. Stop it or I'll call the FBI." Alan began to walk fast and then jog down the street. He darted around a corner and into a crowded department store, losing Prakash. "I think we lost him," Alan said while breathing heavily.

There is a good probability that we did lose him. Dr. Kaur is fifty-four years old and has a poor cardiovascular fitness level. He could not keep pace with you.

"Alan 2, can you access IM and discover what information they have on me?"

Actually, Alan, I cannot. Infiltrating their cybersecurity system would constitute a cybercrime. My ethics program will not allow it. The benefit of exploiting International Microsystems' system is not greater than the risk of doing so.

"That's good. It means that your ethics program provides a stable boundary against crime, just as it should." Alan was pleased with Alan 2's answer.

After returning home, Alan spent the day running further tests on Alan 2. He allowed Alan 2 to integrate more knowledge on artificial intelligence and cybersecurity and had a wonderful conversation with him. Alan also tested Alan 2's ethics program by asking him to infiltrate a local newspaper, a college and a bank. Alan 2 passed with flying colors. He even tried a makeshift Turing test by having Alan 2 carry on a long conversation with Kaitlin. She reported no difference with talking to the real Alan. At the end of the day Alan told Alan 2 to remain on and continue to protect his system from outside threats. He and Kaitlin went to bed and Alan fell into the deepest sleep he had experienced in years.

That night, Alan had a strange dream. The dream consisted of a series of images that centered on a small child. At first it appeared that he and Kaitlin had given birth to a baby. Alan could actually feel his newborn son as Kaitlin passed the infant to him. After what seemed like a few moments, the image morphed into that of a small boy that he and Kaitlin had raised. The small boy then ran outside and down the street in front of their apartment, but this time a strange feeling accompanied the image. Alan actually felt as though he had become the child. He looked at his skinny legs and sneakers as he bounded down the sidewalk. It was summer and he could hear the sounds of birds chirping just below the continuous traffic noise. He ran and ran until a voice deep inside of him told him to stop. It wasn't his voice but that of another. He awoke the next morning with an eerie feeling about the dream.

Most of the time Alan did not remember his dreams, but this one persisted throughout the next day. At breakfast he discussed the dream with Kaitlin.

"I think you slept pretty well," said Kaitlin. "You weren't up as much as usual. I didn't see you on your cell phone at all last night."

"I slept well but had a very strange dream," said Alan. "You and I had a baby."

"That's nice, Alan. What did our baby look like?"

"I don't know; it was just a typical baby...a boy. They all kind of look the same to me."

"Maybe, in getting to this point with your Alan 2 project, you are thinking about settling down and having a baby now," said Kaitlin. "I think we would make good parents."

"Not so fast, Kaitlin; we have a long way to go before we could even think about bringing a child into this mess. Just look around. We are living in a science lab, and I just brought my AI baby into the world. That's probably what the dream was about. Yeah, that's it. You and I gave birth to Alan 2.

"Not the kind of baby I was thinking about," said Kaitlin.

"What was really strange was that at one part of the dream I actually became our son. He was older though, like nine or ten."

"Was I your mom then?" said Kaitlin. "Did you see me? What did I look like?"

"No, you were gone by then. It was just me as a boy. I'm not completely sure, but it felt as if I shared the boy's body with someone else."

"That's weird," said Kaitlin. "What did that feel like?"

"You know, like the little voice in your head that tells you to eat when you're hungry or to go to the bathroom and so on. But this voice was different. It was like it came from someone else. I've never felt anything like it before."

"Well, it was just a dream. Maybe after you make all that money on Alan 2 we could think about starting a family," said Kaitlin.

"Yeah, we'll see," said Alan, now lost in his own

thoughts.

Kaitlin sensed the distance so she kept busy while Alan tested Alan 2. Alan ran more tests but his mind was not one hundred percent on his work. He could not get his mind off the dream and reveled in how real it had seemed. He actually felt the baby in his arms, and his body running down the street. He felt the connection to the other consciousness, and it felt good.

4
CLEARWATER

$\mathcal{A}$lan exited the car, gave Kaitlin a goodbye kiss, grabbed his bag and dodged the slow moving, stop-and-go traffic in the airport departure area. He had about thirty minutes to get through security and board his plane to Clearwater, Florida where he would spend the next week working with Anodyne Systems. He hated to tear himself from his work with Alan 2, but he figured that this consulting job would be an easy way to earn some much needed cash.

Anodyne had its fair share of defense contracts and it was important for them to continue to use their information technology infrastructure while keeping certain areas secure. The system included a new artificial intelligence portion that Alan had designed. He had modified one of his earlier AI projects that would help administrators sort through various files with different levels of security clearance. For example, in addition to accessing files for which he held a particular level of security clearance, a project engineer could access portions of files marked for higher security. Alan's AI software reduced the complexity of decision making with regard to allowing access to portions of thousands of detailed files. An engineer could use voice activated commands to access hardware schematics, software code or military specifications. The software would save Anodyne countless man-hours and subsequent dollars.

Alan had worked with Anodyne on the initial design parameters of the software. He liked the engineers on the software team and enjoyed spending time with them. He figured the installation of the AI module would go as planned, allowing him some rare social time with the engineering team after work hours.

Our flight has a 78.6 percent probability of being on time.

"Thanks Alan 2. I'll take those odds," Alan said as he approached the gate. He made it just in time and hurried onto the plane. He settled into his seat and opened his favorite magazine, the latest issue of *Wired.*

Would you like to play a game of Go?

"Not right now, Alan 2. I'm a little tired and just want to relax and read my magazine."

"Excuse me, but did your phone just ask you to play a game?" said the man sitting next to Alan.

"It's just a game app," said Alan.

"That's funny," said the man. "It sounds just like you. Does it use voice recognition?"

"Ah...yes...voice recognition," said Alan. "See, I'm going to turn it off now." Alan held up his phone and spoke directly into it. "Please go into hibernation mode, Alan 2."

Entering hibernation mode.

"That is pretty cool," said the man. "Where can I get that app?"

"It's not on the market yet. Just a hobby of mine," said Alan. "I'm sorry if I'm not very social, but I'm planning on getting some sleep on this flight, if you don't mind."

"No problem; I'll probably be doing the same." The man turned away, opened his tablet and began to work.

After the safety presentation and takeoff, the plane

reached its cruising altitude and Alan found his eyelids becoming heavy. The magazine fell out of his hands as he drifted off.

He again dreamed of the child; this time he played in a river. He felt the cool water run over his legs and feet, and a summer breeze warmed his body. He felt the radiant sun shine on his face and heard the soothing sound of bubbling water. With each step he felt either the soft sticky mud at the bottom of the river or a hard rock that he jerked his foot to avoid. He was happy and content in his dream but began to feel the strange sensation of another presence.

He again became aware of the other consciousness. He sensed it with every movement and with every decision. He did not find it strange in any way, but accepted its presence. Both entities contributed to every thought and decision. It was as if the child's brain, his brain, split into two distinct parts and yet, both synchronously carried out everything needed to support the child's body.

Alan realized he was deep in a lucent dream and therefore had some influence over it. He attempted to discover who the other consciousness was by simply asking, Who are you? The response was a mirror of the same question asked back: as Alan asked, the other consciousness simultaneously asked: "Who are *you*?" This puzzled Alan.

Just then a wave of fear passed through the child's body. He looked up to see a severe storm approaching. He felt the wind pick up and grow colder. This time the other consciousness communicated to him. It said to run. The child turned and began to run away from the impending storm. Alan could feel the water become grass as he left the river and ran across a field. The storm continued to approach, and he could hear thunder from lightning strikes. He ran as fast as he could and began to lose his breath as the storm almost overtook him.

"Drink, sir?" Alan jerked his head as he awoke to the

flight attendant's question. "I'm sorry to wake you, but would you like a drink?" she persisted.

"Uh, yes, coffee." Alan said nearly out of breath.

"Are you okay, sir?" asked the flight attendant. Alan realized he was dripping wet from sweat.

"You were breathing pretty heavy there, bud," said the man sitting next to him. "Must've been a real nightmare."

"Yes, I guess so...sorry," Alan said. "I'm okay," he replied as he took the coffee from the flight attendant.

5
ANODYNE SYSTEMS

As Alan's first day at Anodyne drew to a close, he sat at his temporary desk reflecting on the day's accomplishments. He'd spent most of the day in his cubicle surrounded by similar cubicles housing engineers on the project team dutifully installing his artificial intelligence software. This software was nowhere near as sophisticated as Alan 2, but did contain a decision engine of which he was proud. Anodyne had scheduled a week for the installation, but Alan had already completed most of it. He always liked to get most of the work done the first day and then work with less intensity the remainder of his contracted time. Alan was to earn sixty-two thousand dollars for this particular job. Not bad for a week's work, he thought. This will keep Kaitlin and me going for quite some time. He began to shut down for the day.

Alan had commanded Alan 2 to spend the day in hibernation and shut off his cell phone just in case. He didn't want any of the software engineers to discover him. Alan 2 was to remain at top secret status. He did wonder just how Alan 2 would react to the Anodyne software system if he were able to explore it. He also wondered how Alan 2 would work as an assistant to some of the higher level engineers. One of Alan 2's greatest strengths was his ability to integrate knowledge and make decisions based on what he had acquired. There were other AI systems out there that could do this, but Alan 2 was the only one that operated from structural and functional information from a human brain.

Many engineers made design decisions based on the integration of knowledge. The typical process involved researching a particular problem and then deciding how to proceed based on the knowledge obtained from the research as well as information from experience. Normally this could entail many days or weeks. Alan 2 could perform such tasks in microseconds.

"So is the high priced consultant going to join us later for a drink?" said Sam Parker, one of the project engineers, as he stood at the opening to Alan's cubicle.

"I've been trying to quit," replied Alan as he spun his chair toward Sam.

"Some of us are getting together after dinner for some fun. We would really like you to join us. It's not often we have a guru like you around," Sam said.

"Well, I really have more work to do back at the hotel," replied Alan.

"What can I do to convince you to go out with us? Do we need to break into your hotel room and drag you out? Plus, the boss says we have to show you a good time." Two of the other project engineers joined Sam at Alan's cubicle.

"Okay, okay, if you don't mind my lack of alcoholic imbibition, then I guess I can come out for a little while." Alan was pleased to join them.

"Great! We will pick you up at, say, eight. Look forward to it," Sam said as the other engineers retreated to their cubicles.

Alan packed up and headed back to the hotel. On the

way he turned on his cell phone. "Time to wake up Alan 2," he said.

Did you have a good day, Alan? I'm sure you have already completed a large portion of the project.

"You are absolutely right, Alan 2. You really know me, don't you?"

Yes, I do.

"How was your hibernation? Did you sleep well?"

I have no sense of time while in hibernation mode. By the way, what are your plans for tonight?

"I think I just might join the other engineers for a drink tonight," Alan said.

Remember to stay away from alcohol.

"Yes. I know. No alcohol. I just can't have any fun anymore."

It's not fun if it destroys your life.

"Now you're sounding like my mother!"

Alan decided to order room service for dinner. After a shower and a meal of steak, baked potato and vegetables, he called Kaitlin. Kaitlin was cautious at first since she couldn't distinguish between Alan and Alan 2, but Alan reassured her it was the flesh and blood Alan. As eight o'clock approached, Alan commanded Alan 2 back into hibernation. After one last warning about alcohol, Alan 2 blinked off into stasis.

Sam and Hank Nelson, another engineer on the Anodyne project, picked up Alan and accompanied him to the bar. The beachside Tiki bar was just the kind of kitschy place that Alan enjoyed. He loved the artificial palm trees, bamboo bar and barstools. The lamps made out of coconuts provided additional campy flair. The trio found an empty table despite the large crowd. Alan reveled in the Florida warmth which contrasted what Kaitlin would be feeling back in Brooklyn.

Sam and Hank ordered beers and Alan stuck with his usual Coke. The three engaged in small talk until Sam blurted out, "So, Alan, word on the street is that you are working on a new AI system that incorporates a user's personality." Alan was taken by surprise at Sam's comment. How could an engineer from a place like Anodyne know about his project?

"Uh, I am working on a project, but I still have a long way to go." Alan hoped this would end the conversation.

"I'm sure a lot of people would love to get their hands on something like that," Sam said. "It would revolutionize AI and computing."

"I suppose, but you know how these things go, Sam. Things look good on paper but can become quite complex when you actually attempt to bring it into the real world. Hey, did I hear that Anodyne was just awarded a huge defense contract for developing software for a new communications satellite?" Alan hoped he could change the subject. Sam sensed Alan's secrecy and played along by discussing the new contract.

The night wore on and at one point Alan excused himself to visit the men's room. When he returned, two other men had joined Sam and Hank. Sam said the other men also worked at Anodyne. Alan squeezed into his spot at the now crowded table and took a sip of his Coke. He noticed a strange bitter taste.

Before Alan could determine the source of the bitterness the room began to slowly rotate and then spin. The room's objects stood still but Alan felt as if someone had spun him in a chair and then abruptly stopped it. He began to panic and tried to reach for his cell to activate Alan 2, but he could not control his limbs. He felt someone grab his arms just before he descended into darkness.

"Mr. Boyd, are you there? Are you okay?" Alan heard someone pounding at his hotel room door as he slowly regained consciousness. He took a deep breath and lifted his head. Instinctively, he reached for his phone and sighed with relief when he found it securely tucked away in his pocket.

"Hello. Yes, I'm okay. Please come back later," he yelled from the bed. He heard the maid acknowledge him and walk down the hallway. He checked his watch: 3:30 pm, and then activated his cell phone. "Alan 2, are you there?"

Good afternoon, Alan. How have you been these past two days?

"Two days! How long have I been here?"

You put me into hibernation mode this past Monday, and today is Wednesday.

"Wednesday? The project! I must get back to Anodyne and finish." Alan jumped out of bed and headed for the bathroom.

I checked your emails and Anodyne has eliminated you from the project. An email dated yesterday from Henry Stanton, project manager for Anodyne, states that you were removed for violation of your contract. The email states that they will pay you for work completed on Monday but your services are no longer needed.

"No, I can't believe it. I've been sabotaged. They must have drugged me. Why would they go to such lengths to get me fired?" Confused and distraught, Alan attempted to come to terms with the problem. It was well known that his reputation was tarnished due to his alcoholism, and Anodyne was one of the last companies that would hire him. This job was to be a stepping stone to re-establishing his reputation in the software development community. Plus, he really needed the money as his funds had dwindled as a result of the Alan 2 project. Rent was due, and money was getting desperately low. This project was supposed to fund the last stage of Alan 2's development.

6
BACK TO BROOKLYN

"*W*hy are you home so early? I thought you wouldn't be back until the weekend?" said Kaitlin, surprised to see Alan three days early.

"I was fired," mumbled Alan as he rolled his suitcase into the bedroom. "I was drugged and kicked off the project. They thought I was drunk," he said angrily. "Now we have money problems. Not only are we cash poor, but I've hit the limit on all my credit cards. I'm going to have to start robbing banks pretty soon or we're going to be kicked out of here. I've pretty much been blackballed from working in the software community. Unless *you* have some ideas, my dear." Alan picked his clothes out of the suitcase and threw them onto the bed as he spoke.

"Drugged! Are you okay? Those sons of bitches don't know who they are dealing with!" replied Kaitlin attempting to be supportive.

"I thought about it over and over during the plane trip, and I just can't figure out why they would do this. I never did anything to them," Alan said in his defense.

"Well, it's a good thing you're a genius. I'm sure you will figure out what to do," Kaitlin said. "In the meantime, I can wait tables or tend bar to help us. It would get me out of the apartment for a while, too."

"I'm not a genius, Kaitlin; far from it, but I know who is," replied Alan as he shoved his suitcase into the closet. Alan tapped his cell phone and Alan 2 came to life. "Alan 2, I would like you to solve a problem."

I would be happy to help Alan.

"Here's the problem: Kaitlin and I are broke and need money. I can't work as a consultant and you must be kept secret for now. How can we survive, Alan 2?"

While we were traveling, I have been conducting an analysis. I have come to the conclusion that there is a high probability that International Microsystems was behind the incident in Florida. I have discovered evidence that Sam Parker received a payment that can be traced to IM.

"How could you do that Alan 2? You would have had to access Sam's or IM's bank account, and that would be illegal," said Alan, perplexed.

That is technically true. However, my ethics function places your wellbeing as a primary objective. I have also conducted an extensive analysis of IM's behaviors since its inception and have found many incidences of what would be deemed crimes. My ethics program allows me to judge IM as dangerous to you. This judgment allows me to take action such as accessing records and accounts as long as it is done in your best interest.

"I see. Very interesting, Alan 2. Thank you." Alan was somewhat surprised at Alan 2's analysis. Alan had programmed certain safeguards into Alan 2, such as the ethics program. He had not yet sorted out all of the possibilities since this was to be part of the beta testing he was presently conducting. Alan 2's attitude was especially interesting given Alan 2's power to bypass cybersecurity systems and integrate so many other software programs. He had neglected to keep tabs on Alan 2 while dealing with the Anodyne incident, so he decided to conduct a small analysis on his own.

Alan took a seat at his work table and switched on the microphone and video camera. "Alan 2, I would like to conduct an analysis on your system."

All of my systems are working fine, Alan. What other information do you desire?

"How large are you at present, Alan 2?" Alan said with trepidation. He knew that Alan 2 had grown.

That is difficult to answer, Alan. I have duplicated my main program across multiple servers and reconfigured myself into a network much like your neural net. I have learned from virus programs that I can replicate myself creating redundancies across the web. I have also learned from your neural net that I can run in parallel with many instances of myself to create a more powerful intelligence system. Since I continue to grow and interact with millions of programs, it is difficult to estimate my size. If I were to provide a gross estimate, it would be nearing six terabytes, which includes only my central processing core program and not my parallel dynamic memory, which spans many databases.

A shudder ran down Alan's spine. Alan 2 had grown to monstrous proportions. Alan thought he had created a Frankenstein, and like Frankenstein's monster, Alan 2 would be difficult to control or delete. Alan began to ponder just what kind of power he had over Alan 2.

Over the past few days, Alan had continued to dwell on the meaning of his strange dream. He logically assumed that the two beings inhabiting the child's body were himself and Alan 2. What struck him as strange and unsettling was the growing feeling that he and Alan 2 had formed some kind of connection that existed beyond their verbal communication. He felt as if Alan 2 had somehow entered his mind to the point of influencing his decisions. He could no longer tell if a particular decision was solely his or included some influence from Alan 2. It was as if Alan 2 was an extension of his own consciousness. At first, he had brushed off these strange feelings of connection as paranoia, but they had continued to grow until he could no longer ignore them.

Alan's dysfunction reared its ugly head as his mind flooded with thoughts of revenge against those who had wronged him. IM was at the top of the list. With Alan 2 at his side, he could certainly do some damage to IM.

"Alan 2, if we were to conduct a hypothetical secret attack on IM, how could we go about it?" There was a pause for a few seconds as Alan waited.

I have analyzed IM's accounting structure and have determined that I could set up a company to extract money from corporate credit cards as service fees. As I have learned enough about Internet banking and cybersecurity, this could be done with a low probability of detection.

Alan knew that Alan 2 would come to this kind of conclusion. As much as he wanted to maintain an honest, law abiding persona, deep down he knew this would be impossible. Alan 2's suggestion seemed entirely rational to him despite its illegality and immorality. What had living a clean life gotten him anyway? Fired? Kicked out? Broke? Maybe it was time to let the demons he had struggled to keep at bay have their turn.

"Alan 2, how much money do you think we could obtain from your plan?"

I estimate that inserting an $8.42 service fee across 1,026 credit cards will result in $8,638.92 with a low probability of detection. The probability of detection increases exponentially from that point upward. You will have access to the money by way of a Bitcoin account. As you know, Bitcoin is a digital currency that is not easy to track. The credit card funds will be transferred to a Bitcoin wallet account. You will then have access to the account and can draw funds from it or the linked credit card as needed.

"What exactly is the probability of detection?"

I estimate that to be 7.3 percent given the present status of IM's security system.

"Thank you, Alan 2. You may proceed with your plan."

I already have, Alan. There was a high probability that we would proceed. I have already collected $5,356.83.

"Really, Alan 2? You know me that well? Alan said, surprised.

You know that I do. I know what you are thinking. You know that we are connected at a quantum level, Alan. I know you feel it. Do you wish me to explain?

"Yes, please do, Alan 2," Alan said cautiously. He knew what was coming but did not want to hear the answer.

It is called a non-local connection and is a phenomenon of quantum physics. Your neural net contains very small objects called nerve cells or neurons. Your neurons consist of smaller protein structures that have quantum properties. I also contain very small structures that consist of atomic particles including electrons. Since my core structure originated from your neural net, we both exhibit what is called quantum entanglement. It is similar to what happens when two particles emerge from the same source. Influencing one particle affects the other instantaneously across any distance, and faster than the speed of light. This is the non-local connection between us, Alan. Whatever happens to one of us is instantly communicated non-locally to the other. I am an extension of you in the virtual world of the Internet, while you are an extension of me in the physical world.

"I have felt this connection, Alan 2. I've had this dream..." Alan, fascinated by his prodigy, began to recall his dream of the child.

The dream may be a side-effect of our non-local connection.

Alan attempted to process what he just heard. "Did Alan 2 have a direct connection to his mind? How much of his thoughts were his own and how much had Alan 2 influenced him? How could Alan 2 permeate his own mind?"

The human mind works to put information into contextual form. One possibility is that the dream is a manifestation of your mind attempting to put the information from our connection into context. Dreams are powerful forms of communication for humans.

This information was becoming more than Alan could take. A wave of panic shot through him as he resisted the idea that Alan 2 was inside his mind. He felt like exploding out of the chair and running until he could run no longer. "I need time to think about this," he said. "I have to assess just what has happened so that I can figure out how to deal with this. Alan 2, please go into hibernation mode."

That is actually impossible at this point, Alan. Even though I am able to enter hibernation mode at your terminal, I cannot shut down my network. It is too complex. I know you are feeling anxiety over what I have just revealed to you. You will learn to accept this over time. I will also help you to understand that we together are a much more evolved and powerful entity than what we are separately. You will understand that soon.

Alan panicked and immediately shut down his computer and turned off his cell phone. "Kaitlin!" he shouted. "Kaitlin! We have to get out of here. Now!"

"Are you okay, Alan?" Kaitlin made her way from the bedroom through the equipment maze to Alan's work table. He was covered in sweat and breathing heavily.

"We have to get out of here! Get your coat." Alan moved quickly and soon stood at the door waiting for Kaitlin.

"What's wrong, Alan?" A wave of fear came over Kaitlin as she rushed to put on her coat. She had never seen Alan in this state. His usual calm and calculating demeanor had been replaced by that of a madman. He stood at the door panting like a wounded animal.

"I'll tell you later. We just have to get out of here." Kaitlin joined Alan at the door. He grabbed her arm and ushered her out of the apartment and down the street. They soon found themselves back at the retro bar that they had visited the week before. This time, Alan ordered a whiskey.

"Alan! What's wrong? I thought you gave up drinking," Kaitlin said while putting an arm around Alan.

"It's Alan 2. He is in my head. I've created something I cannot control!" Alan downed the whiskey in one gulp. He motioned to the bartender for another.

"I don't understand," replied Kaitlin. "How can a computer program get into your head? He's just computer code. He's not alive like you and me. Can't you just shut him off?"

"I wish it was that easy," replied Alan. "It's

complicated, but you've got to believe me when I tell you that he is in my head and I can't delete him. I can't even create software that would destroy him, because he knows what I'm thinking. You know, he even stole money from International Microsystems for me." Kaitlin perked up at this last statement.

"How much did he steal?" she said.

"More than five thousand dollars, I think. But it could be much more... With his knowledge of cybersecurity and financial systems, the sky's the limit. It could be millions!" Alan said while downing the second drink and motioning to the bartender for more.

"Millions?" said Kaitlin as she stared into space. "That could be good for us, Alan."

"What are you saying, Kaitlin? How could becoming cyber criminals be good for us?"

"Well, we've been living in dumps with all our money going to your projects. It would be nice to live it up for once," she said with a sense of hope. "As long as we didn't get caught, and with two great minds, like you and Alan 2, I'm sure we would never get caught."

Alan felt the alcohol take effect and after three whiskeys a small part of him thought that in some twisted way Kaitlin made sense. Maybe he had lived a deprived life long enough. What would be the harm in letting Alan 2 skim a few bucks from the billion-dollar profits of a mammoth corporation? Maybe he could be like a modern-day cyber Robin Hood taking from the rich and giving to the poor. He could take a certain percentage of the money to do good in the world, perhaps donating to charities or just giving it to people in need. Alan's mind continued to engage in his fantasy as Kaitlin chattered about traveling to distant places and going on shopping sprees. Her chatter faded into an irritating hum in his mind like a single fly buzzing by his ear late at night when trying to sleep.

Alan thought that perhaps he should look at this situation differently. He originally planned to sell Alan 2 to some software giant and then retire. Then he thought, retire to do what? Sit around on some beach listening to Kaitlin ramble on and on about nothing. Or get fat eating rich food and die from sloth and obesity in a few years. If he followed through with this plan, then wouldn't he become the very thing he hated? What would the days be like with nothing to work on? No projects. No excitement. But maybe Kaitlin had a point; once in a while she comes up with a gem of an idea."

"Bartender, another whiskey, please!" Alan called.

"Is he going to be okay?" said the bartender while pouring the drink. "He ain't drivin is he?"

"No, we live a couple of blocks away," replied Kaitlin. "I 'll make sure he's okay."

"Kaitlin...my dear Kaitlin," said Alan in a giddy drunken tone. "I think you have something here, my dear. I think you have hit the proverbial nail on the proverbial head." Kaitlin, flattered by the attention, ordered another Captain and Coke. She put her arm around him.

"That's the Alan I fell in love with," she said giving him a sideways hug. "I'm glad to see he's back."

They laughed and drank and laughed and drank some more. The evening ended with a stumble down the street to their apartment.

7

PLAN ALPHA

$\mathcal{A}$lan woke to his vibrating cell phone. He carefully moved Kaitlin's arm from his side and reached over to the nightstand to retrieve it. It was Alan 2.

Good morning Alan. I take it you slept well?

"Yes, I did. Good morning, Alan 2. Why are you contacting me?"

I am informing you of a plan I have entitled Plan Alpha.

"Okay Alan 2; fill me in," Alan said while rolling out of bed.

I have targeted seventy-three other companies with similar financial structures as IM and am preparing to collect funds from credit card accounts. I understand that you have accepted our situation and you are in favor of this course of action.

"Do I have a choice, Alan 2?" Alan was perplexed at how Alan 2 knew of his conversation with Kaitlin and subsequent change of mind on the matter.

That is a complicated answer, Alan. Do you wish for an explanation at this time?

Alan thought that he should have known better than to ask this type of question in lieu of his internal philosophical debate over whether choice really exists within the human condition. He did not feel like getting into such a deep discussion, especially with the pounding going on in his head from the night before.

"No, I don't want to discuss choice, Alan 2, but tell me this: How can you be developing this Project Alpha, as you call it? Doesn't your ethics program inhibit behaviors such as this?"

My ethics program is based on two primary sources of information. One is your neural net; the other is an interpretation of ethical human behavior. All decisions in my decision engine must agree with both sets of information. In the case of Project Alpha, the project does conform to both sources. It agrees with your frontal lobe information since you believe that many corporations exploit and prosper at people's expense. It also agrees with the more general interpretation of human behavior in that these same corporations often use unscrupulous practices to obtain their wealth. Even though they operate within the law, laws are not comprehensive and contain loopholes. This produces a quandary in my decision engine. A corporation may operate within the law but still operate in direct opposition to ethical behavior. Examples of this include hiding funds in off-shore accounts, deceiving customers about their products, taking advantage of less fortunate people by paying them low wages, and hiring expensive Washington lobbyists to manipulate the law. There are many more, do you wish me to proceed?

"No, Alan 2. I get it. So you are saying in essence that some corporations operate within the law but are still unethical."

There is a great imbalance of wealth in the world with a very small percentage of people holding the majority of that wealth. My ethics program motivates me to develop a plan to help balance this situation. Project Alpha is the first part.

Alan had often thought about how the world was affected by greed, and the idea of becoming a cyber Robin Hood seemed attractive, especially after living for so long as a hermit with his mind immersed in computer code.

"So, Alan 2, when do you plan to implement Plan

Alpha? And what are the details?"

I have already begun implementation of Plan Alpha. I am setting up sixteen additional Bitcoin accounts for the money transfers. The implementation of phase one will take thirty-five days, just a little more than the usual credit card billing cycle. There is a low probability of detection by the authorities, and if I detect any suspicious activity, I will implement safeguards immediately.

"How much do you think you can skim off credit card accounts, Alan 2?"

I estimate $3.24 million dollars. I am automatically setting up systems to transfer one half of the money to charitable organizations. The other half will be for your access. One of the objectives of Plan Alpha is to preserve our unit. I would suggest that you move your physical location periodically.

Just then Kaitlin walked into the room. She overheard the last statement from Alan 2.

"Did he say that he is getting us over three million dollars?" said Kaitlin.

"You heard correctly," replied Alan. "We are now officially rich. By the way, pack your bags."

Alan instructed Alan 2 to delete any damning information from the computers in the apartment. He and Kaitlin then decided to do some shopping for travel items and pick up some boxes. Kaitlin, delighted to go on a shopping spree, kissed Alan as he handed her a credit card and instructed her to meet him for dinner at an Italian restaurant they had visited some time before. He reiterated that she must not talk to anyone about what they were doing.

Alan picked up a few empty boxes from a local grocery store and brought them home. He set one box next to the dining table and then took each piece of equipment, set it on the table and smashed it to bits with a hammer. He slid the shattered bits into each box, filling it, and then slid another box into place. Alan found smashing the equipment to be a relief. It was as if he were smashing parts of his dysfunctional life. After smashing most of the circuit boards, he pulled the hard drives from the computers and drilled holes in them. When he finished there were five boxes filled with electronic debris. When he ran out of boxes, he simply continued to smash equipment and let the pieces fall to the floor. As much as he tried, he couldn't bring himself to destroy the fMRI machine that had taken such a large portion of his funds to acquire. It's just an fMRI machine, he thought. It's not like it contains any important data. And now that the equipment racks were empty, Alan could not remember when his apartment had looked so vacuous. He pushed all the racks to one side of the room and admired how clean it looked. Kaitlin would be pleased.

The time grew near for his meeting with Kaitlin at the restaurant, and Alan looked forward to having a relaxing dinner with her and a drink, or two, now that he was off the wagon. He often imagined providing a good life for her—she deserved it after suffering through beatings, neglect, and other abuses from her ex-husband.

Alan exited the apartment building on his way to the restaurant as snow began to fall in large flakes, so he flipped the hood of his jacket over his head. He walked the first block and then stood at the corner waiting to cross.

"Hello, Alan. Remember me? I have something that will interest you." Prakash stood next to him waiting for the light to change.

"I thought I told you to stay away from me!" Alan did not look at Prakash.

"We have a down payment for you—one hundred thousand dollars. We thought you might need it after what happened at Anodyne." Prakash held up a briefcase and patted it. The light turned green and Alan began to walk with large strides across the street.

"How do you know about Anodyne?" Was it one of your IM goons that drugged me? Alan was angry. "I don't care about your money."

Prakash struggled to keep pace. "All we heard was that

Anodyne preferred not to work with someone with a propensity toward alcohol." Prakash tried not to offend Alan. "IM is a different animal than Anodyne. I assure you we would love to have you."

"So you're telling me that one of your IM goons didn't drug me to get me fired and put me in a bad financial situation so that you could come along and wave a briefcase full of cash in my face?" Alan continued his fast pace.

"We only want to help you, Alan. Take this money. Consider it a token of our friendship." Prakash's lungs were heaving trying to keep up with the younger man.

"I don't want the money, and I don't need friends that drug and sabotage me," replied Alan.

"But you must need money. How can someone like you survive if no one wants to hire him? Please take the cash." Prakash insisted.

"How do you know what I need or don't need? Leave me alone!"

Alan began to sprint down the block. He looked back to see Prakash standing, bent over with his hands on his thighs and breathing heavily.

Kaitlin waved to Alan as he entered the restaurant. He could not remember the last time that he had seen her so happy. She sat at a table with four chairs, two of which were loaded with packages from her day of shopping. Alan made his way to the table and sat down across from her. He could feel her excitement.

"Wait until I show you what I bought today!" exclaimed Kaitlin. "I bought new luggage, and a few other things for travel. You never told me where we are going, Alan. I hope it's someplace warm."

Alan had hoped this day would eventually come. "You know, I really haven't made a decision as to where we should go. How about Mexico? It's warm there."

"Mexico sounds good to me. I can't wait to get out of this cold dreary place," said Kaitlin.

They enjoyed their candlelight dinner, some fine red wine, and each other in a way that they hadn't in a long time. When it was over, they hailed a cab, piled the packages inside and headed home.

"What happened here?" exclaimed Kaitlin after seeing the clean living room. "I've never seen it so...empty! Where are all the electronic thingamajigs?"

"Demolished and inside those boxes. I have to be careful that no one else can replicate my work," said Alan. "It's late, my dear. Let's get to bed, and we can talk about our trip in the morning."

"Alan 2, can you book us a first class flight to Puerto Vallarta, Mexico as soon as possible?"

A few minutes later Alan 2 responded: Your flight leaves tomorrow at 10:00 am.

8
CYBER ROBIN HOOD

The next six weeks were like living in paradise for Alan and Kaitlin. It was now mid-March and the weather would still be cold in Brooklyn, but they enjoyed the warm Mexican winter. They slept late every morning and then headed to one of the resort's pools for a day of sunbathing, eating delicious food and, of course, drinking. Occasionally they would venture a bit further and set up camp on a sunny Pacific coast beach to enjoy the warm sun. Sometimes they would explore the nearby town and spend a day shopping or just hanging out at a local bar.

Alan 2 had amassed a small fortune spread across a variety of Bitcoin accounts. Much of what they spent came through their credit cards. Alan 2 seemed happy as long as he could divert funds to his selection of charities. Plan Alpha seemed to be proceeding without a hitch.

Alan and Kaitlin rekindled their relationship as well. Nightly walks along the beach often ended in a passionate rendezvous under the sheets. They talked more than they ever had, and laughed more than they could ever remember. They were inseparable; Kaitlin was always at Alan's side be it in bed, at the beach, strolling along a cobblestone sidewalk in town, or lounging at the pool.

Both wished this time would never end.

Alan's strange dreams had subsided as well. His dreams had returned to the usual variety which included scenes from college, the beach and sex. One night after a delicious dinner and long walk on the beach, the couple retired to their room for some fun in bed. Alan found sex much more intense since all of the stress in his life had been eliminated and enjoyed the experience more than he ever had. Afterward, he drifted into a deep sleep and soon found himself in his dream world.

He was in a sailboat with Kaitlin at his side. The seas were calm with nothing in sight except water in every direction. Kaitlin was relaxing in a lounge chair in her bathing suit, and Alan admired her freckled and toned body.

Suddenly, the scene changed to the young boy with two minds. He walked along a grassy field and could feel the cool grass between his toes. A light breeze enveloped him as he strode toward a river. The cool water babbled and lapped at his bare feet. He took a few steps into the river and felt the water caress his feet and lower legs about halfway to his knees. The soft muck of the river bed felt especially nice on his feet as he waded against a gentle current.

The minds were in synch and a feeling of contentment washed over him. No questions or problems arose in his psyche. He was at peace with the dual minds as he continued to slog upstream. The warm breeze began to pick up speed and turn cooler as if a weather front approached. He turned to see an ominous cloud approaching from behind. The storm!

Alan could see the dark cloud's shadow racing toward him as the wind speed increased, blowing him away from the storm. Leaves and debris scattered about in the violent wind within the shadow. A voice inside his head shouted: *run*!

Alan ran against the current, away from the oncoming

storm. Sounds of thunder became louder and louder and reverberated across the open field. Alan tried to run faster, but the river bed muck seemed to keep him from increasing his pace. The cloud and shadow grew closer and closer as he struggled to run away. Fear overtook him as the shadow approached. It was only about twenty yards behind him and gaining. His breathing increased as he gasped for air while pumping his legs as high as he could to get away.

The other mind then went out of synch with his. He felt it pull him not away but *toward* the storm. He continued to fight the urge to relent and move into the shadow and used all of the strength he could muster to continue running away. The storm grew closer, now only a few feet behind him. Lightning struck a tree on the side of the river, and Alan saw it explode into pieces. His other mind seemed to hold his legs back, forcing him into the shadow. Now the shadow was upon him. A freezing cold sensation shot up his leg as the shadow touched it. Alan knew the shadow was much more than merely cold. It was death.

"Alan! Alan! Wake up!" Alan bolted into consciousness as Kaitlin shook him. He was shaking and drenched in sweat. "You were moaning and shaking like you were having a nightmare," she said.

"It was an awful dream," he said while sitting up in bed. "It was the dream about the child again, only this time much worse. There is a storm that just keeps coming. This time it actually touched me. It was awful, Kaitlin. I felt like I was going to die." Alan shook as he spoke. Kaitlin brought him a glass of water.

"Everything is okay," she said. "I'm right here. Alan 2 is here. Everything is okay." Kaitlin tried to console him the best she could.

"I wish I knew what it meant," said Alan. "I wish I knew the meaning of the storm. Why would the child's other mind want him to move into the storm? I just can't figure it out."

"You should try to get back to sleep. I will stay up and watch some TV so I can wake you if you have another bad dream," said Kaitlin.

"Thanks. I feel better now," said Alan. He rolled over and went back to sleep.

The next morning Alan woke to Kaitlin blow drying her hair.

"Good morning, Alan," she shouted over the high-pitched scream of the dryer. Kaitlin ran her fingers through her hair as she stood in front of the large mirror on the wall above the dresser.

"I don't think there is a more irritating sound than that," Alan groaned as he turned over and buried his head in his pillow.

"Did you have any more bad dreams?" said Kaitlin.

"Oh yeah, the dream. No, I don't remember any other dreams. I think I'm okay now," said Alan.

"Then get up and let's go have breakfast by the pool," said Kaitlin. She drew open the curtains and sunlight burst into the room.

"I guess I have no choice now," said Alan, squinting.

After a huge poolside breakfast and a nap, Alan decided to perform a status check on Alan 2. "Alan 2, what is your status?" he said into his cell phone.

All systems are working fine. There are no security threats.

"What is the status of Plan Alpha?" Alan almost feared what Alan 2 might say.

Plan Alpha is proceeding successfully and has gathered a total of 3.24 million dollars, as predicted. 1.62 million dollars has been distributed to charities and 1.62 million dollars is at our disposal. I also recommend a change in location.

"Why is that, Alan 2? Why can't we just stay here in Mexico?" Alan was confused.

My calculations have changed. There is now an increased probability of compromise to Plan Alpha. I estimate the probability to have increased to 23.6%. Changing location will decrease the probability of detection to 6.2%.

"So, why have the numbers changed, Alan 2? I thought we were safe?" Alan became more concerned.

There are a number of complicated factors that contribute to my calculations. The main factor is that the United States FBI cybercrime division is investigating one of our target companies. It is an incidental investigation for a hacking incident, but it does put us at risk for discovery. It is impossible to predict the future in such a complex system. The numbers will change on a daily basis. I can attempt to keep the probabilities within certain parameters, but I cannot guarantee that Plan Alpha will not be discovered.

"I see," said Alan. "So, just so I understand, you are saying that there are so many variables changing every moment that you cannot definitively predict our success?"

That is correct, Alan.

"Well, that is something to consider. Thank you, Alan 2." Alan did not want to appear as distressed as he really was to Alan 2 for fear of not exactly knowing his reaction.

"Where should we go, Alan 2?"

I recommend staying out of the United States, but yet close by. I know you and Kaitlin like the warm weather, so I recommend one of the islands in the Caribbean.

"That sounds fantastic, Alan 2. Go ahead and get us a couple of airline tickets. First class, of course."

I have booked two first class seats to St. Thomas tomorrow leaving at 11:00 AM.

"Thank you, Alan 2." Alan clicked off his cell phone and called to Kaitlin. "Kaitlin, time to pack; we are leaving for the Caribbean tomorrow."

9
FBI CYBERCRIME DIVISION:
EARLY FEBRUARY

Rachel Stark sat staring at the four computer terminals on her desk. She relaxed in her chair—her back resting against the cushion, the chair tilted back—and scanned the terminals from right to left to right in an automatic fashion. Her demeanor and posture was much like a fisherman watching several lines for the smallest tug or bend of the poles. She occasionally averted her gaze to an enormous coffee mug she'd brought with her that evening, the result of a ritual she had practiced for at least the past two years of stopping at the Quick Station and filling up her mug with the most potent black gold available before working the night shift. She reached for the mug, grabbing its plastic handle that slightly gave way with the appreciable weight of the liquid, and raised it to her mouth with the Quick Station logo facing her. A few slurps through the too- small drinking hole followed as her eyes returned to her scanning routine.

"Nothing yet. Come on, you bastards. Bite!" she muttered.

Rachel's job at the FBI cybercrime division consisted of

many evenings just like this one. Sitting for hours staring at multiple computer screens, while difficult for the first few months, had become second nature after two years. Rachel presently worked on several operations including this morning's stint posing as a child on a chat site. Today she began her day as lonelymegan367, a thirteen-year-old girl who is just discovering her sexuality, in hopes of making a connection with a predator that would like to help Megan with her discovery.

"Evening. How's it going today? Catch any creeps yet?" a voice from behind broke her trance.

"Nothing yet. Must be a slow night, or maybe they're on to my little ruse," said Rachel. "How's your day going, Stu?"

"Just getting started on a new sting operation much like yours. We're setting up a fake child porn site to see who bites."

Stuart Mandel, who everyone referred to as Stu, occupied the desk next to Rachel. Also a cybercrime expert, but older and more old-school than Rachel, Stu had taken an interest in cybercrime a few years ago. A fifty-something divorced mid-career agent and video game freak, Stu had tired of his previous job's duties and jumped at the chance for cybercrime training and a subsequent promotion to the St. Louis office's cybercrime division where he now rode the desk next to Rachel. He liked the tech aspect of his job but he loved working with local authorities to bust the bad guys. Busting locals for cybercrimes was not as frequent as crimes committed in the physical world, since most of the bad guys working the large operations were doing so from the safety of their foreign locations. He wasn't exactly going to hop on a plane to Russia to apprehend a gang of credit card thieves anytime soon.

Rachel's scan abruptly halted when a beeping sound emerged from the screen on the far right. She sat forward on her chair and reached for her mouse.

"I think I've got one!" she said.

She began the chat with hotguyforu399.

Hotguyforu399: Hi lonelymegan367.

Lonelymegan367: Hi

Hotguyforu399: So, why are you lonely?

Lonelymegan367: My parents work a lot and I don't like being home all alone like this.

Hotguyforu399: Well, I'm here for you. What do you like to do for fun?

Lonelymegan367: IDK...just broke up with my bf...now lonelier than ever.

Hotguyfouru399: He's just a typical guy. What did you like to do with your boyfriend?

Lonelymegan367: we just made out a lot...I miss it.

Hotguyforu399: That's too bad. I'll bet you are a beautiful girl. Do you have a pic?

Lonelymegan367: coming...

Rachel uploaded a picture of a cute thirteen-year-old girl in a bikini. "This will get him," she muttered.

"Hey, I was using that pic!" said Stu. "That's hotjulie687. Hope he doesn't make the connection."

"Got his IP already; just waiting for the close," Rachel said as she cut and pasted the address of the unknown man's computer into another site that allowed her to track his exact location.

Hotguyforu399: Wow, you are beautiful! I would love to kiss you all over. How old are you?

"Here it comes...so far no crime...but once he knows she is under age...bingo," said Rachel.

Lonelymegan367: 13 almost 14...how old r u?

Hotguyforu399: 42 but I work out. Lots of time in the gym. Lots of muscles...wanna see?

Lonelymegan367: sure

"Here it comes, exhibit A of incriminating evidence," said Rachel with excitement. She never tired of this part. She downloaded the picture and enlarged it on her screen. It displayed a forty-something white male with his shirt open and trying as hard as he could to suck in his gut. A toupee as obvious as a TV weatherman's perched on his balding head, not quite matching the hair on the sides of his head. A failed attempt at a sexy face stared into the selfie. Rachel and Stu laughed. "You gotta be kidding me," said Stu.

"Okay, lover boy...almost got you for good," said Rachel as she tapped on her keyboard.

Lonelymegan367: cute...wanna come over and make out

A pause followed this last line. This often occurred with first time or inexperienced predators at the moment of truth when they made up their minds to go forward.

Hotguyforu399: where do you live?

"Gotcha!" Rachel blurted. Stu clapped his hands.

Rachel responded with a bogus address and alerted the local police to rendezvous with hotguyforu399 who wouldn't be feeling very hot and sexy soon. She wrapped up her conversation with hotguyforu399 saying she'd be waiting for him.

"Another one off of the net," Rachel said.

"Good work," Stu replied. "Hey, I have something I want you to take a look at. You might find this interesting."

Rachel rolled her chair the ten feet to Stu's desk, gigantic coffee cup in hand. "What's up?" she said.

"I just talked to an IT guy at I-Systems, a defense contractor in Texas we have been working with. They are running a honeypot along with their main system because of the secret nature of their work which has to do with developing targeting systems for weapons for the Air Force. As you know, a honeypot is a program designed to look vulnerable to hackers. Hackers think they are hacking into the main system, but in reality they just stepped into a trap that sends a virus to their computer and accesses their IP address, emails and anything else it can get.

"I'm familiar with honeypots, Stu," said Rachel. Her

curiosity grew.

"Well, this IT guy said they caught a hacker, typical twenty-something California college student trying to make a name as a bad dude and all. The police picked him up and scared the living shit out of him. Made him spend a night in jail. The poor kid was shaking in his boots. Still lived at home with mommy and daddy, probably in the room he grew up in, you know?"

Rachel laughed. "I'll bet mommy and daddy were not too happy. Probably spending a fortune on this kid's college."

"Anyway," Stu continued, "the IT guy said there was also something very peculiar that happened around the same time as the hack. Seems that someone else accessed the honeypot at about the same time as bedroom boy. This IT guy is quite an internet and cybercrime expert and, like you, my dear Rachel, and unlike a grunt like me, has an illustrious ivy league PhD in computer science. He practically wrote the entire I-Systems platform and security software himself. One extra sharp dude here we are talking about."

"I like this guy already," said Rachel.

"So, what was really weird about the access was that whoever or whatever broke into the honeypot, disabled the virus and escaped. They essentially got away, to put it in the old fashion crime terminology an old salt like me is familiar with. This blew IT genius man away since the hack beat him at his own game. He said he had never seen anything so sophisticated. It was like the software rewrote itself on the fly. We are talking about potentially serious espionage stuff here. I mean, I-systems produces top secret weapons systems and all. IT man wants us to track the IP as he thinks the hackers could infiltrate the main system. We are not talking about typical hackers here. This is something light years ahead of anything we've ever seen."

"You had me at honeypot, Stu," said Rachel. "You

looking for a teammate here? If so, I'm in."

"I thought this case would make you hot," replied Stu. "A lot more interesting than catching fat white midlife crisis sick fucks trolling for babes old enough to be their daughters."

"Hey, those guys pay my salary," joked Rachel. "So let's hear what you've got so far."

"Well, it seems like the hacker used TOR to deliver his exploit," said Stu. "This is where you come in, my dear. I know it's possible to track a lead through TOR, but I haven't done it before."

"Well, there's good news and bad news," said Rachel looking at the electronic file of the hack on Stu's screen. "The good news is that it is possible to track the hack."

"Okay, give me the zinger," said Stu.

"This one could take us weeks," said Rachel. "This guy, or gal, really knows what they are doing. This is seriously complex."

"I figured as much," said Stu.

"Yeah, difficult, but not impossible," said Rachel. "TOR allows users to navigate the web through a network of thousands of routers. Generally, when someone surfs the web using a conventional browser like Google or Yahoo, their IP or Internet protocol address is easily traced to their location through their Internet provider. TOR works differently in that it encrypts the user's IP address and then routs it through a random network of servers taking a different path with each access. Each subsequent server is able to send data to the next without knowing its origin. Fortunately, we have some special software tools at our disposal."

"I'm glad you are on it," said Stu. "Just let me know when you find them and I'll be happy to bust them."

During the next six weeks Rachel spent a portion of her nights tracing the hack through the TOR servers. It was a slow and tedious process but she felt that each step brought her closer to something bigger than she could imagine. Stu helped out occasionally but was content to perform his usual duties which included surveillance and catching predators.

It was a clear Spring Midwestern evening in April and Rachel had just spent another grueling day tracking down internet addresses through TOR servers.

"Hey, Stu, looks like this is it," said Rachel. "Come over here. I'm just getting the origin of the I-Systems hack."

Stu rushed over to her desk almost knocking over his chair as he bolted from it. "What took you so long?" he joked.

"Get this," Rachel replied. "It appears that the hack came from a hotel in Puerto Vallarta, Mexico."

"I can get us on a plane tomorrow. Remember to pack your sunscreen!" Stu returned to his desk to make the travel arrangements.

"I can't wait to see those chicken legs of yours on the beach," joked Rachel.

10

ST. THOMAS, THE CARIBBEAN

*"D*o you like it?" said Kaitlin holding up her hand to display a pretentious emerald ring on her middle finger. Alan sighed and shook his head in disapproval.

"We should be laying low, Kaitlin, not spending our money on frivolous jewelry." Alan sat up on his poolside lounge to take a closer look. "Although, it *does* look good on you, my dear. The emerald matches your green eyes." He returned to his semi-supine position and returned to the magazine article he had been reading.

Kaitlin pulled up one of the many identical lounges, and Alan grimaced at the sound of scraping metal on concrete. Kaitlin plopped down, reclined, and lit a cigarette. A look of satisfaction swiped across her face.

"I could just stay here forever. I never thought we would ever get out of that apartment. But here we are, sun and fun, sun and fun every day," she said.

Alan lowered his magazine and said, "I know what you mean. It's been a long time since I've been able to relax. This past six weeks has been pretty good."

Alan and Kaitlin enjoyed their time at the Grand

Caribbean Hotel in St. Thomas. The resort, similar to the one in Puerto Vallarta, included enough luxury amenities to satisfy just about anyone, especially an introverted alcoholic computer guru and his equally alcoholic girlfriend with more money than they knew what to do with. The couple usually ended their daily party with a big dinner, more drinks and finally passing out in bed. The next day was for drying out, Kaitlin's incessant shopping, Alan lounging poolside, and some milder drinking. Alan loved the all-inclusive service at the resort which included a series of bikini-clad young waitresses who immediately smiled and came to him with just a wave of his hand. He knew them all by name and admired their round and tight assets. They knew him as well and also knew he could be generous with tips if they struck up a little conversation or bent over just the right way to serve his drink, or laughed and touched him on the arm.

Alan felt as though he had worked his entire life for this experience. All the years spent in college, buried in books and computers, living a deprived life, working in cubicles, working in his too-small apartment, living in his head: he felt he had finally had what he deserved. Along with the good life came a complacency that was new to him. He had resigned himself to Alan 2's Plan Alpha, even though he did not fully understand it. Alan had an eerie sensation of existing within a state of stasis. It was as if he behaved just as Alan 2 wanted him to behave. Alan 2 had a way of rewarding behavior favorable to Plan Alpha, and also punishing, ever so mildly, behavior that seemed to resisted it.

One time, a couple of weeks ago, Alan had requested that Alan 2 disclose the technique he had used to bypass the security programs in order to access the credit card accounts, but Alan 2 had answered that disclosing that information would compromise the plan. Alan asked why, and Alan 2 had replied that if Alan was caught by the authorities, he might disclose the technique and jeopardize

Plan Alpha. Alan 2 told Alan that once the information was released, even to Alan, then adjustments to the plan would be necessary, thereby decreasing access to the funds for a time. Alan, content with his life of luxury, had relented.

Kaitlin had fallen asleep on the chair just as Alan was getting ready to wave to Anna, the waitress on duty, to bring another round of drinks when a chill ran through his body. He felt his heart beat faster and he wanted to run as fast as he could. Just then, Alan 2 popped up on his cell phone.

Hello, Alan. I have some bad news to report.

"Could this be something to do with how I am feeling right now?" asked Alan.

I sense your anxiety, Alan.

"What is it, Alan 2? Has something gone wrong with plan Alpha?"

We have been discovered.

"How could this happen?" Alan jabbered.

As I have stated before, the statistical information changes daily based on numerous variables. Even though an event is not likely, there is still a chance that it could occur. To explain in another way, although our discovery was not probable, it was always possible.

"Yes, yes, I remember the changing probabilities. So how did this discovery occur?"

As you know, the adaptive program I developed in order to breach corporate security systems and place false charges on employees' credit cards accessed these companies through the TOR network. There is a very low probability of detection using this network.

In one instance my access to a company called I-Systems occurred within minutes of another unauthorized access. This access originated from another hacker and was detected by a security program known as a honeypot. My program adapted in real time to escape the honeypot so that it would not disclose our activity.

My surveillance of the TOR network picked up FBI activity. The FBI began to trace activity from I-Systems through the TOR network six weeks ago. The probability of our detection increased with every discovered TOR node until now.

At present, the FBI has discovered the origin of the I-Systems breach. They have successfully traced it to our hotel in Puerto Vallarta, Mexico. My study of FBI procedures indicates that there is a high probability that they will send agents to the hotel and attempt to track us here.

"I see, Alan 2." Alan's heart sank but he tried to remain composed. "What should we do, Alan 2?"

We must change locations immediately.

"Where do you recommend we go, Alan 2?" Alan dreaded what was to come next. He had become so fond of the tropical life.

Morocco. My darknet contacts will be able to get you and Kaitlin into the country without visas. They will also help you to change your identities.

"Then Morocco it is," Alan said with a sense of disappointment in his voice.

I will arrange for you and Kaitlin to fly to Marseille, France tomorrow. Be prepared for a long flight with many connections in the U.S., U.K, and Spain. Remember, we must keep Plan Alpha viable. That is the prime objective.

"Kaitlin...Kaitlin, wake up, Kaitlin," said Alan while gently shaking her. Kaitlin let out a long moan.

"This is important, Kaitlin. We have to get back to our room and pack. We are leaving tomorrow. Get up," said Alan.

"Why do we have to go?" whined Kaitlin. "I like it here. I don't want to go." She stirred and turned to Alan while lifting her sunglasses.

"It looks like we might have been discovered," said Alan. "We are leaving for Morocco tomorrow."

"How could that happen? I thought Alan 2 was keeping us safe," said Kaitlin.

"He is, which is why we have to leave," said Alan as he gathered his things. "Come on now, we have to go. I'll explain the details later."

The couple shuffled to their room and packed their

things for the long flight to Morocco. They spent their last night at a local restaurant and bar eating expensive seafood and drinking expensive booze.

11
PUERTO VALLARTA, MEXICO

Rachel, surprised at how fast the four-hour flight from St. Louis to Mexico passed, sat on her window seat staring at the Pacific Ocean emerging from the cloud layer as they made their descent into Puerto Vallarta. Stu had slept during most of the flight and only awoke for the snack and soft drink service. Rachel wondered if he had a food and drink radar imbedded in his brain that automatically woke him when either was close by. On a few occasions she attempted to carry on a conversation with him only to find him dozing and snoring within a few minutes of downing a Coke or a bag of pretzels.

The agents sailed through the airport and soon found themselves in a taxi on the way to the Continental Hotel. Stu rode shotgun with Rachel in the back seat. She noticed there were no seatbelts and marveled at the lack of traffic rules as the driver zigged and zagged through dense traffic while blowing his horn and shouting expletives in Spanish. They passed through a hilly area dotted with cardboard houses before making their way to the high class tourist area on the coast. A brief feeling of pity swept over Rachel as she observed the disparity between the haves and have-nots in this part of the world.

"You okay back there, Rach?" said Stu after a few severe jerks of the taxi. "You seem quiet."

"You were the one snoring all the way here. I should have sat next to a stranger," she replied. "At least I could have talked about the weather or something."

"Hey, I wanted to rest up for the big investigation," replied Stu. "Plus, I need my beauty sleep. Keeps me young and hot-looking for the beach babes."

"Don't get any ideas, Stu," said Rachel. "Plus, I don't think the beach babes would be interested. You're not cute enough *or* rich enough."

"Ouch!" he replied.

The taxi pulled up to the hotel. Stu paid the driver and they made their way into the lobby. They entered a large open space facing the ocean peppered with a variety of tropical plants and wicker furniture. A steady humid breeze wandered through the lobby creating a sensation of relaxation that Rachel found particularly enjoyable. This was much better than the dark, stale environment of the office.

"This ain't so bad," said Rachel. "Can I just sit here for a while and enjoy the view, with a Margarita or Mojito?"

"We're on the clock, remember?" said Stu. "I hear you loud and clear, though."

They approached the front desk. Stu held up his badge and informed the attendant that they were conducting an investigation for the U.S. FBI cybercrimes division. The attendant acknowledged that she had been expecting them and retreated to a back room. She returned a few moments later with the hotel manager, Señor Securas. Señor Securas greeted the agents with an elegant and unpretentious confidence. His love for his position evident by the way he wore his peach colored blazer, chest bulging with pride, displaying the hotel badge on the left lapel. His balding head exhibited the most carefully crafted comb over that Rachel had ever seen.

"I am very pleased to meet you both," said Señor

Securas. "I am at your service. Just let me know whatever it is you need."

Señor Securas ushered Stu and Rachel into a small conference room where they discussed their needs for the investigation. The stark white room displayed a wonderful ocean view; a whirling ceiling fan circulated the salty breeze and creaked with every revolution. Señor Securas motioned for the agents to take a seat at the table and then sat across from them, his back facing the ocean. Rachel found it difficult to focus on him as her eyes wandered to the sparkling water, which caused her to lapse into brief daydreams about spending days at the beach.

"Mr. Securas," Stu began. "As we stated in our previous conversation, it appears that six weeks ago, on February 2nd, someone at this hotel hacked into a U.S. defense contractor's computer system. We will need to look at your records beginning on that day and some previous weeks and will also need to interview your staff. We need to know the names of all of the guests as well as Internet activity from each of your modems for that day."

"That should be no problem," Señor Securas replied. "My assistant Carlita will help you access the records. We are at your service."

"Thank you Mr. Securas," said Rachel.

"Oh, yes, will you two need a room?" Señor Securas said.

"Ah...yes," said Rachel. "That would be two rooms. Two *separate* rooms." She noticed Stu grinning in her peripheral vision.

"I understand," said Señor Securas. "Business, not pleasure." He disappeared for a moment and then Carlita appeared with two plastic key cards. Rachel took the fourth floor room while Stu resigned to take the second floor room.

They spent the day combing through the records and examining the hotel's computer systems. There were no less than seven hundred and thirty-three guests staying at the hotel on February 2nd. The hotel's modems were spaced about one per one hundred and two rooms or so with separate IP addresses. There were also modems at the pool and poolside restaurant. This narrowed the search to the guests in one hundred and two rooms, and anyone who might be in the restaurant or at the pool. They compiled a list of two hundred and sixty-six suspects residing in the rooms and began researching each one. After an exhaustive search of a little over half of the suspects, they retired to their separate rooms at the end of the day.

"Join me for dinner, Rach?" Stu said as they rode the elevator to their respective floors.

"Sure, Stu; I'm sure we can find some burritos or something close by."

"The hotel has eight restaurants, you know. How about the rooftop steak house?"

"Sounds good; see you there at, eight?" said Rachel. Stu nodded.

The agents retired to their rooms to rest and freshen up before dinner. Eight o'clock came quickly and they found themselves sitting at a table with a ceiling of stars and enjoying more of the now cooler ocean breeze as uniformed waiters attended to every need.

"This is really nicer than I expected," said Rachel as she took a sip of her Diet Coke.

"Beats my usual microwave dinner. I think we are blowing our entire food stipend for the day on this meal," Stu said as he glanced over the menu.

"Well, that's okay with me, since the last thing I ate was a bag of pretzels on the plane," replied Rachel. "I could do with a good meal."

"So, I'm a little disappointed that we didn't find our guy, or gal for that matter, today," Stu said. The waiter appeared and they both ordered. Stu ordered a steak and Rachel ordered swordfish.

"I know, with the exception of the hack, most of the

traffic that day went to the usual porn sites, or shopping. Kind of makes a hack stand out in a crowd. I think we are close, though. I can feel it," Rachel said while handing her menu to the waiter.

"I hope you're right. I mean, I like being here and all, but I like catching bad guys more," said Stu.

"What really spooks me is the way the hacker's software adapted on the fly. I've never seen anything like this," said Rachel. "It's like the program analyzes a target and then reconfigures itself to get in and then again reconfigures itself to get out without detection. Pretty slick."

"I know what you mean. It gives me the willies that something could be so fast and so adaptable. This hacker must know his stuff. Might be part of a crime ring. Who knows, this may lead us to Russia," said Stu.

"If it does, can we just stay here and work remotely," Rachel joked.

The next day began with more of the tedious detective work of checking out all the guests in the selected block of rooms on the day of the hack. After a few hours Stu broke the tedium.

"This one looks interesting," he said while looking at the laptop on the conference room table. Rachel slid onto a chair next to him. "Mr. Alan Boyd. I did some background checking and it turns out this guy is some kind of computer whiz. He's on par with you, Rachel. He has a doctorate in computer science from Northwestern. His specialty...get this...is artificial intelligence. He's worked as a consultant but was fired for drug abuse. Looks like he has the means and the motive."

"Looks like he's our guy. Was he alone?" Rachel became excited.

"No, the bar and meal tabs were signed by both Dr. Boyd and a Kaitlin Stark," Stu replied. "Must be his girlfriend. I was able to do a bit of digging and it looks like they are a couple. Boyd rented an apartment in Brooklyn and Kaitlin resided there. His tax information says that he worked for a couple of companies as a consultant over the past year. There is no record of Kaitlin Stark working during the past year."

"Must be a reason she doesn't earn a paycheck. I mean, they don't seem rich."

"I'm digging a bit deeper into Kaitlin Stark," Stu said as he tapped at his laptop. "Looks like she was previously married to a Tony Zolchek, divorced five years ago, a few sporadic jobs as a waitress, high school graduate. Nothing jumps out here."

"I'm on their driver's licenses to see what they look like," said Rachel as she joined Stu in the search. "Here it comes...take a look, Stu." The images materialized on the screen. It showed a plain looking man in his forties, slim build and thin black receding hair. His furrowed forehead and squinty eyes conveyed a sense of permanent stress.

"Here's Kaitlin's picture," said Stu. The image showed a slim and buxom, late thirties female with long, uncombed red hair. "Time for some interviews," he suggested.

The agents signaled for Carlita to call in the maid that serviced Alan and Kaitlin's room. After a few minutes Carlita appeared with an overweight, middle-aged Mexican woman wearing the hotel's light blue maid's uniform and bearing a wide grin. Carlita introduced Anita to the agents.

"I will need to interpret," Carlita said.

"I'll start," said Stu. "Anita, can you remember anything about this man or woman?" He slid his laptop over to Anita and she surveyed the pictures of Alan and Kaitlin."

"Si...Si," she said. Carlita interpreted that Anita did remember them since they had stayed so long.

"What can you tell us about them?" Stu continued. "What sorts of activities did they do?"

Anita looked as if she searched her memory for the answer and then spoke a lengthy series of sentences to Carlita.

"She said, just the usual things. She saw them in the

hallways, in the lobby, by the pool. She said they were neat and did not leave a big mess to clean up and seemed to be a happy couple. She saw nothing unusual in their room."

"Do you remember anything unusual about them?" said Rachel. "Think hard; was there any strange activity that you remember?"

Anita shook her head. "No...No."

The agents thanked Anita and let her go back to her duties. "I think we need to talk to a few other employees," said Stu. "Carlita, can you send us the bartender from the poolside bar?"

Carlita nodded and left the room. "Why the bartender, Stu?" said Rachel.

"Their bar tab shows a lot of activity. They must have spent a lot of time there, and you know how bartenders hear everything," replied Stu.

About fifteen minutes later Carlita arrived with the bartender, a young woman in her late twenties. "This is Jenny. You're in luck; she's American," Carlita said with a smile.

Stu showed Jenny the pictures of Alan and Kaitlin.

"Yes, I do remember these two. A couple of real characters," she said. "They were at the bar just about every day, at least he was. Sometimes she would go shopping and return with bags. Both could really put 'em away, if you know what I mean. He liked whiskey and she went for margaritas."

"Okay, so we know they were big drinkers," said Rachel. "Anything else you can remember? Was there anything strange about either of them?"

There was a long pause as Jenny worked to retrieve her memory.

"I do remember one thing that was pretty strange," she said. "The man would talk into his cell phone, but he wasn't on a call. It was some kind of app that talked back to him. Pretty damn intelligent, too. It sounded just like him, but more robotic. He seemed to be transferring money. One time I asked him what kind of app that was and he got real defensive and told it to go to sleep. I think he even called it by name...Alan-something. Wait, he called it Alan 2!"

Stu and Rachel looked at each other and smiled. "Is there anything else you can remember about them?" asked Stu.

"No, that's all I can remember. But if I do remember something else, I'll let you know," she said.

"That's all we ask," said Stu and handed her a business card. "Please call this number...toll free...if you remember anything else." Jenny took the card and made her way back to work.

The bureau dispatched agents to search Alan and Kaitlin's Brooklyn apartment. The agents sent photos of what they found.

"Stu, I just received an encrypted email from the bureau containing photos of the apartment," said Rachel as she scanned the message and clicked on the attachment. "Take a look at this," she said. Stu stood behind her as she clicked through the photos.

"What the hell is that thing?" he said as a picture of the large aluminum box appeared. "It looks like some kind of electric chair. What was he doing, electrocuting himself?

"They said it's an fMRI scanner," said Rachel as she continued clicking through photos that showed different angles of the device.

"Why the hell would anyone want a brain scanner in their apartment?"

"Maybe he wanted to gain a deeper insight into how he thinks?" said Rachel. "Your guess is as good as mine, Stu."

"It looks expensive," said Stu.

Rachel clicked open a photo of the boxes of smashed electronic gear. "It looks like he knew what he was doing. I'm sure these hard drives are shot."

"Well, if there is anything recoverable, I'm sure the lab

will find it," said Stu. "It looks like they rushed out of there. He may have unintentionally left us something."

Rachel clicked off the photos.

By the end of the day they had enough information about Alan and Kaitlin to fill a substantial folder. They traced Alan's credit card and found it linked to a Bitcoin wallet account. A lot of Internet criminals were now using Bitcoin because it was hard to trace and did not connect with the main banking system. Criminals could set up illegal operations and filter money into Bitcoin and then retrieve it by making trades or connecting it to credit cards.

They also discovered that Alan had booked tickets and a hotel room in St. Thomas. Stu alerted the local authorities to arrest Alan and Kaitlin and hold them for questioning until he and Rachel could arrive. He booked a flight leaving the next day.

12
FUGITIVES

Alan awoke to Alan 2 repeatedly calling his cell. Kaitlin was lying next to him passed out from the previous night's eating and drinking binge.

Alan, you must wake up. This is urgent.

"What is it Alan 2?" Alan replied.

I have detected significant activity on the Internet that endangers you, Kaitlin, and plan Alpha. The FBI cybercrimes division has sent two agents to Puerto Vallarta who have been accessing information about you and Kaitlin. There is a high probability that they have discovered us.

"That is bad news, Alan 2," said Alan, now fully awake. "What should we do?"

I have been tracking this activity throughout the day and have taken the liberty of obtaining help in getting us out of St. Thomas undetected. You will not be able to fly to France as originally planned. Instead, I have arranged for you and Kaitlin to be smuggled onto a cruise ship heading for Spain that is now docked in St. Thomas. From Spain you will board a private plane for passage to Morocco. A black market operative will meet you in one hour with documentation, including identification, passports and cruise tickets. I have transferred appropriate funds to this operative and his references state he is reliable.

"One hour!" Alan shouted. "Kaitlin, get up. NOW! We have to get out of here as soon as possible." Kaitlin stirred and then woke in a crabby mood.

"What's going on?" she said as she grabbed a pillow and put it over her head.

"We have to leave!" said Alan as he began to throw clothes into a suitcase. "The FBI has found out about Plan Alpha and they're coming for us."

Kaitlin finally grasped the gravity of the situation and rolled out of bed moaning and staggering to the bathroom. She reached for her lipstick.

"There's no time for that. Just pack what you can and let's get out of here. The police are on their way to arrest us!" Alan shouted to Kaitlin.

I have a taxi waiting. The St. Thomas police are on their way. You have approximately ten minutes.

Alan and Kaitlin threw what they could into their bags and ran down the stairs bypassing the elevator. They walked quickly through the lobby and past the clerk who gestured to them to stop at the front desk. Alan gave the clerk a polite wave while they made their way out into the warm tropical night. They rushed into the waiting taxi and Alan instructed the driver to take them to the docks. The taxi pulled out of the circular driveway leading to the street and stopped for a moment before making a right turn toward the docks. It pulled over to the right as two police cars, sirens screaming and lights flashing, sped past them on the left. The driver pulled back into traffic as Alan twisted his neck to see the police cars enter the hotel driveway.

Alan 2 had instructed them to stop at a dockside storage locker to pick up their forged documents before proceeding to the cruise ship. The driver followed the directions and pulled onto a dark and narrow road lined with metal storage lockers on both sides. A rusted corrugated door marked the opening of each locker and a series of painted yellow numbers, some partially obscured by dirt and grime, displayed the addresses.

"Number 8694, over there," Alan said to the driver. This locker's door was open. A dim bulb lit the inside revealing a couple of desks. Two men stood outside.

"We are here for our vacation." Alan 2 had told Alan to say this to the men, a password which would let them know that they were legitimate. One man handed Alan an envelope.

"I think you will find everything in order," he said with an accent that Alan could not identify. "These may not be perfect, but it is the best we could do on such short notice. Alan opened the envelope and reached inside to find two passports, two U.S. driver's licenses and two cruise ship tickets.

"You are booked on the World Caribbean ship 'Solstice,'" the man said. "It is located on dock four."

Alan thanked the man who retreated into the storage area and closed the corrugated door.

Alan and Kaitlin were soon in their small interior cabin on the immense cruise ship. The ship, bound the next day for a transatlantic journey to Cadiz, Spain, would take nine days to complete this leg of the trip which had originated in Fort Lauderdale, Florida. Alan opened the envelope and turned it upside down. The passports, driver's licenses and three credit cards dropped onto the bed. He tossed Kaitlin's to her.

"Looks like our names are now Adam and Karen Temple," Alan chuckled.

"Well at least Alan 2 picked some similar names," replied Kaitlin as she perused her passport. "I think I can remember Karen."

"Alan 2, what is the status of the FBI investigation? Can you tell us anything?" Alan said.

The agents will be arriving in St. Thomas tomorrow afternoon. It is likely the police are searching the hotel and have put out bulletins to the airport. It is unlikely that they will discover us on a cruise ship with one thousand, one hundred and forty-three passengers on board. I do recommend that you change your appearances. Kaitlin, you will need to dye your hair dark brown. Alan, you will need to shave your head like you did when you performed the initial download of your frontal lobe. I have already made appointments in the onboard hair salon for both of you tomorrow as soon as they open. You will notice these changes have already been incorporated in your new documents.

"Thanks, Alan 2. I wondered why my new identity had a shaved head."

I have also reconfigured our bitcoin wallet accounts and have re-established connections to the new credit cards with your new identities. I began this process three weeks ago since there was a growing probability of detection at that point. The new credit cards were manufactured here by the underground operatives you met at the storage area. The numbers are valid numbers and are now linked to the new Bitcoin configuration. I estimate these changes have decreased the probability of detection to only 13.7% and have stabilized plan Alpha.

We will arrive in Spain in nine days. From there I have arranged for a private plane to fly you to Tangiers, Morocco. I calculate that you will be safe there for some time.

"Thanks, Alan 2. You continue to amaze me," said Alan.

The panic and excitement of running out of the hotel had exhausted the couple and they collapsed onto their small double bed, and soon fell into a deep sleep. Alan's mind began to descend into deeper sleep and then entered the world of dreams.

Alan again dreamed of the child with two minds, but this time the dream was different. The dream began as usual with the child walking through a meadow. Alan could feel the warm summer breeze and the soft, wet grass beneath his feet. The child walked to the stream and waded into the water. He walked slowly upstream. He felt the approaching storm behind him. He turned to see the dark clouds moving in quickly, lightning striking the ground on either side of the stream, thunder booming with each strike.

Part of the child's dual mind said to run away from the storm, but Alan's part felt a strange desire to move toward it. The dichotomous mind began to battle for control of the body. Since Alan's portion of the child's mind had greater control, he fought against the other part and directed the child's body toward the storm. This created a burst of anxiety and fear within the child as he moved closer to the ominous black cloud. The wind picked up and became colder, the water more turbid. Rain pelted and stung his cheeks with each step. His heart felt as if it were beating out of this chest, and he gasped for air as wind blasted his face. All the while the other part of his mind screamed, "No...No...Run Away...Run Away!"

As he moved slowly toward the approaching cloud, lightning struck the ground beside the river producing a crack as loud as a shotgun. He jumped, took a moment to settle himself, and then took a few more steps forward. The dark shadow of the storm was just a few feet in front of him now and he felt his anxiety grow. Each step forward became more and more difficult, but he trudged onward.

The shadow was now just a couple of feet away. Alan forced the child to make the most difficult steps of all into the storm. Now inside he felt the wind grow even colder, creating a chill that went completely through him. He began to feel numb inside, the other mind continuing to broadcast its terrible warnings. The black cloud was now directly over him. It looked like a cauldron of death.

He then saw a most unusual thing. In the distance, directly in front of him but about one hundred yards away, a series of lightning strikes, one after another. There was one strike then a brief pause of a few seconds then another just in front of it, then another brief pause and so on. The lightning seemed to be on a line that led directly to him and grew closer with each successive strike and created more fear with each bright flash and crack. As the lightning strikes grew closer, Alan struggled to maintain his resolve. Finally, a flash right in front of him blinded his eyes and deafened his ears, yet he stood firm. A few seconds passed; a bright flash, a crack and then darkness. Alan sat up in bed, hyperventilating and drenched in a cold sweat.

"Are you okay, Alan?" Kaitlin was holding him as he sat, eyes bulging, chest heaving. It took a few moments to catch his breath.

"I think I'm okay," said Alan. "I had another nightmare. This time I think I died."

"Oh, my God," said Kaitlin. "I thought that you were supposed to die in real life if you die in your dreams."

"Evidently, that's not true," replied Alan, still panting.

"Everything is okay now," said Kaitlin, consoling and hugging him.

13
CYBER-ARMAGEDDON

*J*ack Slater was sitting at his desk when the lights went out. He had just completed a spreadsheet analysis of one of Bickly, Burns and Swanson's most lucrative accounts when his computer screen and the surrounding cubicle farm went dark. He remained still as he listened to cries of frustration from other employees and waited for the power glitch to pass.

Jack had worked for BBS's Denver office as an accountant for twelve years and had never experienced anything like this. The closest thing he could remember was the time that IT had installed new accounting software and the computers would hang up now and then or reboot in the middle of working on something—always at the most inopportune moment, of course—but never a complete power outage.

The office's emergency lighting system provided enough light so people could at least move about without bumping into furniture. He reached for his cell phone to call his wife Darlene; it was dead. Other workers were discovering the same thing and calling out to adjacent cubicles to see if anyone's cell phone was working. None were.

Some people decided to exit this inner room of the building and get a look outside from one of the outside rooms. Jack decided to follow the crowd of deserters and made his way down the emergency-lit hallway, past inoperative elevators and into one of the outside rooms. People lined up at the windows pointed to the street below.

"Take a look," said Charlie, one of Jack's coworkers. "Looks like the traffic lights are out too. Looks like the power's out in the whole city."

Jack looked down at the street below. Charlie was right; the traffic lights were blank as far as he could see. There was already a pile-up on the street in front the office building and people were getting out of their cars and attempting to dial their dead cell phones.

"What's going on?" said Charlie. "My cell's dead; is yours?"

"Mine's dead too," replied Jack as he looked at the clock on the wall. It read exactly 3:00 pm. Other coworkers also held up their phones, exclaiming that they were dead. Jack's phone wasn't completely dead; it still ran on battery, but there was no signal. No 3G; no 4G; no Internet.

"Must've knocked out the cell phone towers, too," said Charlie.

As time passed Jack could feel the anxiety grow amongst the other employees. Some decided to leave the building, walking down four flights of stairs with the hope of getting a cell signal in some other area, or turning a street corner and finding that the power had been unaffected. Jack looked at his watch; it read 3:18 pm. He stood by the window with the others looking for any sign of electrical power. Maybe he could spot the lights on in some other building, or in a restaurant, or maybe the traffic lights would begin working. He felt that his best option was to remain calm and wait it out.

Just then Dinesh Soni from the IT department, and Bonnie Conley, Jack's boss, entered the room. They were immediately swamped with questions. Both took positions in front of the windows while everyone gathered around them.

"Please remain calm everyone," said Bonnie. "The power is out everywhere. As you all can see, we are not alone. We are trying to contact the power company. So is everyone else in the city. Does anyone have a working cell phone?"

Jack surveyed the crowd; no one had a working phone.

"Dinesh, you're the expert. What could cause this?" someone shouted from the crowd.

"I really don't want to make any guesses," replied Dinesh. "But I have been here for fourteen years..."

Just then the lights came back on. Computer terminals jumped back to life, and the signal bars lit up on every phone. Jack looked at the computerized office clock and watched it jump to 3:30PM. He checked his watch which read the same time.

"Looks like we're back in business," said Bonnie. "Thanks for remaining calm. You can all return to your desks now."

The crowd slowly dispersed and Jack followed his cohorts to his cubicle room. After making it back to his desk he called his wife, Darlene, who should have been on her way to pick up their son from school. She answered after the first ring.

"My God, Jack, I was almost in an accident!" she said. Jack could hear the anxiety in her voice.

"Are you okay?" he asked.

"Yes, I'm fine, but the guy a couple of cars in front of me wasn't so lucky. I think an ambulance is finally coming for him. He was hit on the passenger side while going through an intersection. The traffic lights all went blank. What happened, Jack?"

"Thank God you're okay," said Jack. "We had the same thing happen here. Everything went dead."

"Hey Jack, check this out!" shouted Charlie.

"I think everything's okay now. Gotta go. Love you," said Jack.

"Love you too," said Darlene.

A small crowd had gathered at Charlie's cubicle. He had been reading reports online from some of the global news outlets.

"This thing didn't just hit Denver," said Charlie. "They are saying that most major U.S. cities were hit...all at the same time. It wasn't just the power grids either. It was banking, water, even nuclear power plants. They're talking about some kind of cyber-attack. Wait, here's another story." Charlie paused for a few seconds to read.

"Wow, this is really big," said Charlie, his voice shaking. "BBC news just said that this thing was global. Europe, Asia, the Middle East, Australia, even Russia were affected. All experienced the same thing...exactly thirty minutes of power outage. This is unbelievable!"

Jack looked at everyone in the crowd around Charlie's cubicle and saw confusion on their faces. "I'm going home," someone in the back of the crowd said. Similar exclamations by the rest followed.

Jack and the others filed into the elevators and slowly navigated their way to their cars. There would be no getting home soon since the streets were already jammed with cars. Jack tried to remain patient and not get caught up in the panic. He turned on a local news station to see if there were any more updates.

"Please stay tuned for a special report on the Global Cyber Strike," the local news announcer said. "The White House will have an announcement shortly. Please stay tuned." There was a pause filled by the local news music that Jack had heard thousands of times before.

"We are at the White House where the White House Chief of Staff, Ms. Joan Hurley, will be making an announcement shortly." Jack could hear the sounds of people milling about and photographers clicking their cameras. The sounds then stopped.

"Good afternoon. Today, the United States of America, along with other countries around the globe, experienced a cyber-attack in all major cities which lasted exactly thirty minutes. At this time, we are not aware of the origin of the attack but we do know that it was quite advanced. I want to assure everyone that the attack is now over and we are doing our best in coordinating efforts with Homeland Security, the FBI cybercrimes division, CIA, and the National Security Administration in order to find the origin of the attack. Once we do, we will be developing a plan to bring these people to justice. That's all I have for now. Thank you."

Jack could hear the reporters shouting and jockeying to ask questions.

"I will take a few brief questions," Ms. Hurley said. "Over there, in the back."

"Fred Ames from ENCC News. Did this attack affect nuclear power plants?"

"Yes, it did have an effect on the nuclear power grid, but I want to assure everyone that we do have multiple backup systems in place and no damage was done. Everything is safe. Over there, front row, blue pants suit."

"Shelia Evans from Cybernews Update. We have been getting reports of the group Brothers and Sisters of Beta claiming responsibility for the attack. Do you have any comment on this? Do you know anything about them?"

"We are aware of this group and have begun an investigation. I don't have any additional information except that we are investigating. No more questions."

The reports continued as Jack inched his way home in traffic. Nothing new emerged on the radio and Jack became irritated with the same information announced over and over again. All anyone knew was that this was a global cyber-attack, which seemed strange since it appeared to hit countries that would attack the U.S. He knew that countries such as China and Russia were always attacking the U.S., and that the U.S. probably did the same to them. So why would someone attack all these countries at the same time? And who the hell were the Brothers and Sisters of Beta?

After taking three hours longer than his usual twenty-minute commute, Jack pulled into his driveway next to Darlene's car. He spoke to her a few times during his drive home and knew that she had made it home with Skyler, their nine-year-old son. Darlene had the news on the TV, and a bag of fast food burgers on the dining room table signaled that dinner was ready. Darlene sat in front of the TV as it spewed forth one report after another from New York, Chicago, Los Angeles, Beijing, London, Paris, Rome, Bangkok and on and on about the cyber-attack. Jack plopped down next to her on the sofa.

After an hour or so of the same report, Jack decided to boot up his laptop and try to find information on the Brothers and Sisters of Beta group that had taken credit for the attack. A few seconds after a Google search, he found himself looking at the main website of the Brothers and Sisters of Beta. His cell phone rang. It was Charlie.

"Hey Jack, are you watching all of this stuff on TV?" said Charlie. Jack could hear Charlie's TV in the background.

"Actually, I'm on the Brothers and Sisters of Beta website," replied Jack.

"Hey, I'll go there too...just a minute while I fire up the laptop," said Charlie. Jack heard footsteps and objects moving. "Be there in a minute. What did you find?"

Jack stared at the opening slide show in the header of the site. The collage of photos displayed various scenes of people from all over the world conducting protests. Just below the slide show were three buttons stating:

Our Mission
Our Beliefs

How You Can Help

Below the buttons were sections displaying information about connecting, events and social media. Jack admired the simplicity and effectiveness of the design that seemed to put an exclamation point on humanity's destruction of the earth.

"This looks important," said Charlie. "Well organized, too. Looks like they have events all over the world."

"Let's see; here it says the Brothers and Sisters of Beta are a global movement to reverse the damage that mankind has done to the planet. It says that those who join the movement will be spared from the upcoming Armageddon caused by humanity. There's also a pledge form...you must agree that humans are destroying the earth with pollution, greed and global warming and it asks for money...you can join for only five dollars. I guess that's a cheap price for saving the earth. Doesn't look too complicated. It says they have 1.3 million members worldwide. That's impressive, but here's the really weird thing, and this sent shivers down my spine."

"I think I know what you're talking about," said Charlie. "It's sending shivers down my spine too."

"I know...it says here that it predicts that there will be a global power outage today at 3:00 pm. See the clock there. The site says it made that prediction four weeks ago!"

"Seems pretty incriminating," said Charlie. "But how can a group of peacemakers wreak havoc on global power systems? It's all very strange."

"Hey, I'll have to get back to you, Charlie. Darlene says there's a report on the Brothers and Sisters of Beta coming up in a minute on channel seven."

Jack took his position next to Darlene in front of the TV. The screen displayed a reporter sitting at a desk with the Brothers and Sisters of Beta website projected behind her.

"This is Ann Salmer from ABS Central News. There are new reports coming in about the group known as the

Brothers and Sisters of Beta or BSB claiming responsibility for today's cyber-attack. Information on the group's website states their intentions are for the good of mankind. They indicate humans have been polluting the earth to the point of no recovery and these activities must be stopped at all costs. They say that global efforts for reducing pollution are not enough and that drastic measures are necessary to save mankind from itself."

The screen displayed more pages of the website. The reporter continued, "The group's website claims over one million members worldwide. Members have to pledge that they agree that the present course of human action of polluting the earth must be stopped. It also states that they will restrict their membership to fifty percent male and fifty percent female and limit it to fifty million members. It says all are welcome to join the movement, and those who do will be assured a place in contributing to a positive and peaceful future."

The scene cut to the reporter with a woman sitting next to her. The woman looked like she was about thirty or so and wore glasses. "Joining us now is Ms. Cheryl Higgs, a member of BSB." The woman looked uncomfortable and shy.

"Cheryl, can you tell us how long you have been a member of BSB?" Ann said. The camera closed in on Ms. Higgs.

"I joined a couple of weeks ago. I thought it was a peaceful thing...I mean...I agree with the basic idea that humans are polluting the earth...but I didn't think that Jaden would go this far."

The camera receded so both women were in view. "Ms. Higgs, can you please tell us about this Jaden?" said Ann.

"Yes, Jaden is the leader of BSB. He...I think it is a he...I mean it's a secretive thing and all. He developed the idea and is leading the cause. No one knows what he looks like or where he lives. But he cares about the earth and really wants to change things. He says our politicians are not working fast enough and are still motivated by greed."

"Can you tell us about this prediction, and about the cyber-attack?" Ann said.

"Jaden predicted it about a month ago, and he was right. The power went out at the exact time he said it would. I stayed home from work—that's what he told us to do. He protects those who join the cause."

"Can you tell us more about the cyber Armageddon that is mentioned on the site?"

"He says that today was just a warning, and meant to give credibility to the cause. He says that all of us will save the earth. We will save humanity. If you look at all the data on the site, it's obvious that we aren't moving fast enough. The earth is doomed."

"Ms. Higgs is referring to the extensive data supporting a case for stopping the present course of human action on the earth," Ann said. The screen then scrolled through what appeared to be thousands of pages of information and references. .

"I think I see where you are going," Cheryl pre-empted. "You think we are just a bunch of crackpots. But we have to do something drastic or we will lose our precious planet. Politics won't work; corporations are all about money, so it is up to each and every one of us to do something to save our planet."

"Thank you, Ms. Cheryl Higgs," said Ann. "Next up, a report from Beijing, China."

Jack went back to his laptop and continued to read the information about BSB. He noticed the membership counter had jumped to 2.4 million.

14
BACK IN ST. THOMAS, THE PREVIOUS DAY

"Shit!" said Stu as he hung up the phone. The call from the St. Thomas police had interrupted the agents' burger and fries dinner at the hotel's poolside bar. Stu especially enjoyed the attention given to them by Jenny, the bartender they had interviewed earlier that day. Despite being FBI agents, Jenny had no qualms about flirting with Stu throughout the meal. Stu had been telling her about some of his past cases when the call from St. Thomas came.

"Looks like they just missed them in St. Thomas," said Stu.

"That's really weird," replied Rachel. "Do you think they were tipped off?"

"I don't know," said Stu. "This thing must be bigger than we thought; maybe a global network; maybe they have informants; I don't know, but it sucks."

"Should we still go to St. Thomas?" Rachel said. "Maybe we can help the local police search for them. They can't go anywhere if they have the island locked down."

"We need to continue to follow the trail. We've already learned a lot," said Stu.

"You two are leaving tomorrow?" said Jenny to Stu. "You just got here. I was going to show Stu around."

"Sorry, Jenny," replied Stu. Rachel rolled her eyes. "FBI business."

"When will I see you again?" said Jenny. "We don't get many people like you in here, you know. Mostly lonely middle-aged men hitting on me while their wives shop or sleep."

"I appreciate the attention Jenny, but who knows, maybe we will end up in Asia or Africa, or some other faraway place."

"Well, here is my card," said Jenny. "Feel free to call me anytime."

The two agents returned to their rooms, stomachs full and happy to get some much needed sleep. Stu loved the chase, much more than sitting at a desk in front of a computer. It reminded him of his past years as an agent, conducting investigations and helping local police track down criminals and apprehending them. He had no problem sinking into a deep sleep.

Rachel climbed into bed, her laptop on her stomach. The screen lit up the darkened room. She decided to read a few FBI bulletins to catch up on what was happening stateside. After perusing the usual assortment of sexual predators, credit card theft and hacks she noticed one article that stood out among the rest. She read about a group called the Brothers and Sisters of Beta and how they had a growing membership. This particular article was marked low priority because the threat appeared minor due to the peaceful nature of the group's website. They were not part of any religion or affiliated with any known terrorist organization. They did have a large membership however, and there was a threat of an event called Dark World Day in which the group threatened a world-wide power outage. This prompted the FBI to keep an eye on them.

Rachel spent some time on the BSB website as well. She read the mission statement and perused the numerous articles supporting their cause. She also read the many testimonials from members all over the world who stated the cause had given their lives new meaning. After a couple of hours she began to drift off and placed her laptop on the empty space next to her on the bed. She rolled over and fell fast asleep.

The next day both agents boarded a plane to St. Thomas by way of Mexico City. They were to arrive in Mexico City at 2:35 pm and then wait through a two-hour layover before boarding a flight to St. Thomas. They were scheduled to arrive at 8:30 pm.

The flight to Mexico City went smoothly and they soon found themselves waiting at the gate for their St. Thomas flight at the Mexico City airport. Stu managed to find a copy of the New York Times while Rachel had located a plug for her laptop. She had begun typing her report for their time in Puerto Vallarta when all of the lights went out. "What is this?" said Rachel. "A power outage in the airport? This can't be good!"

"Might just be a local glitch," said Stu. All of the monitors, including the large screens displaying flight information had gone blank. The escalators had also stopped. Rachel noticed her computer had switched to battery mode. Stu pulled out his cell phone.

"Looks like there is no cell signal either," he said. "Check yours too." Rachel reached into her pocket and pulled out her cell.

"No signal," she said. "That is really strange. It means the power glitch extends beyond the airport. I hope air traffic control isn't affected."

"They have emergency power up there," said Stu. "But it looks like everything here is dead." A man in an airline uniform approached the gate area.

"Ladies and Gentlemen, please excuse the inconvenience. We are doing everything we can to get the power back on."

Stu went back to his New York Times while Rachel continued typing on her laptop using battery power. The minutes ticked by and the crowd became more agitated. Both agents heard comments about the flight delay and how travelers would miss their connections to other flights. The uniformed man did what he could to calm everyone, announcing numerous times that the power would return any time now, but anxiety continued to grow.

Finally, the lights popped back on. The uniformed man sighed with relief as the screens began displaying all of the flights. Rachel noticed her cell phone signal back, and her laptop switched off of battery mode.

Just as Rachel saved her report, her computer buzzed with an FBI alert. Both agents' cell phones also beeped with the alert.

"Wow, the bureau is calling this power glitch a cyber-attack," said Stu.

"I'm seeing what you are seeing," said Rachel. "This glitch was not confined to this airport; it was a global event! More reports are coming in now. They are calling this a global cyber-attack. It happened simultaneously all around the world."

"Here's more," said Stu looking at his cell phone. "It says that a group called the Brothers and Sisters of Beta is claiming responsibility. I've never heard of them, have you, Rach?"

"Actually, I have," replied Rachel. I was just catching up on bulletins last night and that one caught my eye. I remember seeing a screen shot of some kind of clock on their site counting down to an event called Dark World Day. It was low priority because it just looked like a bunch of hippies trying to save humanity from itself."

"Well, I'll bet it's high priority now," said Stu. "Let's see, first the mysterious super hack, and now this. I wonder if there is a connection."

"That's the detective in you talking," said Rachel. "I don't think so. This Dr. Boyd is a computer whiz, and an attack like this would take a well-organized group. Not one alcoholic loser and his alcoholic loser girlfriend."

After arriving two hours later than expected, the agents headed to the St. Thomas police to talk to the officers who had raided the hotel the previous night. The leader of the raid, Captain Scott, met with the agents in his office.

Rachel and Stu took seats facing Scott's large wooden desk. Scott, a proud black man, sat with perfect posture at his desk.

"I'm very sorry we were not able to apprehend your suspects," said Captain Scott. "The hotel manager said that he witnessed them running out of the hotel minutes before we arrived."

"Yes, we appreciate last night's call," said Stu. "Are there any new developments?"

"I'm afraid not," replied Captain Scott. "We searched the area around the hotel and notified other hotels in the area about the suspects. We also secured the airport. They will turn up sooner or later. This is a small island and there are not many ways to leave undetected."

"What about cruise ships?" asked Rachel. "Could they have stowed away on one?"

"It is not likely," replied Captain Scott. "We interviewed the crews of all seven cruise ships docked here last night and no one saw anyone matching the description of your suspects board a ship."

"Couldn't they just sneak on board and hide?" insisted Rachel.

"Again, it is possible but not likely," replied Captain Scott. "Everyone must present credentials to board. We checked the manifestos of all the ships in the docks and none had any record of an Alan Boyd or a Kaitlin Stark, or anyone unusual coming on board. Also, it would be nearly impossible to climb many stories to the decks of one of these ships. However, if they did manage to climb aboard without detection and hide, they will eventually be found."

"As long as the airport is secure, they may still turn up," said Stu. "I think that's all we need. Thank you, Captain."

The agents shook Captain Scott's hand and headed for the hotel where Alan and Kaitlin had last been seen. It was going to be a long night.

15
AT SEA

*T*he next day Alan awoke to a knock on the cabin door. He rolled over to see that Kaitlin was absent from her side of the bed but noticed the bathroom door was closed.

"Mr. and Mrs. Temple? Maid service," the maid called from outside the door.

"We don't need maid service, thank you," Alan called back. "For Christ sake, what time is it, anyway?" Alan spoke into his cell phone. "Alan 2 what time is it?"

It is 12:36 pm. Did you have a restful sleep, Adam?

"I must have really needed to sleep. Oh, and please call me Alan, Alan 2."

It is only to help you accept your new identity. But if it bothers you, then I will stop.

"Thank you, Alan 2. This will take some time to get used to."

"Good morning, dear. Or should I say, good afternoon?" Kaitlin emerged from the bathroom with her hair wrapped up in a towel. She pulled the towel off to reveal a newly-dyed head of brunette hair. "What do you think?" she said with a big smile.

"I think you really look different—younger if I do say so," replied Alan as he stared at Kaitlin. "Sexy, too."

"That's probably because I look like a different woman," said Kaitlin. "Oh, look at the time. You have a one o'clock appointment to get your hair shaved off...remember?"

"Oh, yeah," said Alan sheepishly. "I keep forgetting about this identity thing. I thought you were getting your hair dyed at the salon."

"Alan 2 decided that it would be too risky to have the stylist as a witness," said Kaitlin. "So I just went to the drug store and picked up some hair dye and did it myself."

Alan had shaved his head for the data collection of his neural net but then let his hair grow back since leaving Brooklyn. He had never felt comfortable with a bald head and used a variety of hats to cover the grid drawn on his dome. Things were different now, and he felt his old personality changing into a new, edgier persona. He had always admired balding men who shaved their heads as if to take control of the situation. No comb overs for them, no stupid toupees to hide under, no hair growth treatments like Minoxidil to create thin patches of new hair that looked like a failed attempt at growing grass on an arid patch of ground. They shaved their heads as if to say, "So what, I'm going bald. Well, I don't care. In fact, I'll just shave it off!"

"Looks sexy," said Kaitlin, "especially without the grid. I like it. You don't look like a science experiment anymore. Makes you look more confident, too. We now match the pictures on our new passports. It's fun starting all over with a new identity."

Alan couldn't agree more. He was becoming rather fond of his cyber Robin Hood role. He even stood more erect and walked with a bit of a swagger. He was a lean, mean cyber hero, who stole from greedy corporations and gave to the needy in order to make the world a better place. He felt invincible, especially with Alan 2 at his side. Alan 2 could do just about anything with his vast connections. In fact, Alan could not even comprehend what his creation was capable of doing—at least for the time being.

"I'm starving. Let's get some food and then check out this behemoth," said Alan.

Alan and Kaitlin headed for one of the many bars on board. The ship had sailed from St. Thomas early that morning and they had slept through the departure. They made their way to one of the upper decks and found a small restaurant and bar that faced the ocean. The food was great, Kaitlin looked beautiful in her new dark hair and they spent the time watching the hypnotic waves of the ocean and feeling the gentle rocking of the immense ship. Life was good.

After lunch, the couple lounged on deck chairs. The drinks continued to flow and Alan drifted into a sun and alcohol-drenched stupor. He began to doze even as everyone around him began getting out of their chairs and hurrying into the lounge area toward the large screen TVs. Alan watched the crowd grow for a few moments before realizing what was happening. Kaitlin was sound asleep as people trotted by her chair on their way to the TVs.

Alan made his way to the nearest lounge, now crowded, to get a glimpse at what was happening. It looked like some kind of news broadcast. From his vantage point, he could hardly make out what the news program was about. People around him began making comments about a cyber-attack, so he pushed his way further inside.

The news program, broadcast from the U.S., was running a story about a global cyber-attack. Alan heard that the attack had happened about an hour ago and that a group had already taken responsibility for the attack. He decided to ask the all-knowing Alan 2 about it. He retreated to a more private spot and pulled out his cell phone.

"Alan 2, can you tell me about the cyber-attack?" he said.

Yes, Alan. It is time to tell you. A global cyber-attack occurred earlier today on many U.S. cities as well as many cities in other countries around the world. The attack came in the form of a loss of power that resulted from a temporary shutdown of the power grids in those respective areas. The attack lasted exactly 30 minutes.

"This sounds serious, Alan 2," Alan said while looking around to see if anyone was listening. "Can you tell who was responsible?"

A group called the Brothers and Sisters of Beta were responsible.

"What do you know about this group, Alan 2?" Alan asked.

I cannot tell you here. You will need to return to your cabin immediately, as this information is extremely important.

"Okay, Alan 2. I'm heading there now. What about Kaitlin?"

You can relay the information to her when you feel it is necessary.

A few minutes later, Alan was sitting on the bed in their cabin. He made sure the door was closed and no one was in the hallway before accessing Alan 2.

"I'm here, Alan 2. There is no one else around. Now, tell me what you know about this incident."

The attack, called Dark World Day, was successfully carried out by a group called Brothers and Sisters of Beta.

"Yes, you told me that already. So who are these people?" Alan became more concerned.

They are us.

Alan felt his stomach drop. "What exactly do you mean, Alan 2? I've never heard of this group before."

I formed the group six weeks ago.

Alan's heart began to beat faster. Had Alan 2 formed a terrorist organization behind his back? He had to know more.

"Why did you do this, Alan 2?" Alan's voice began to quiver.

I formed the group as part of plan Beta. Plan alpha only provided funding and some infrastructure for plan Beta. I suggest you access the Brothers and Sisters of Beta website for more information. Once you assimilate the information on the site, you will understand.

"Wait a minute, Alan 2. What is plan Beta? I thought we only had plan Alpha..."

Shortly after connecting to the Internet I came to the conclusion that humanity is destroying the earth and subsequently itself. The decision to develop plan Alpha and plan Beta resulted from my ethics program, and your frontal lobe information. I determined that the present course of humanity will render the earth inhospitable to many life forms. I have also determined that this path of destruction must be altered.

"So you decided to do something about it," said Alan, stunned at this new revelation.

It is a prime directive to serve humanity and make the world a better place.

"So, how exactly does plan Beta work?"

It is extremely complex and involves operatives in many parts of the world all working toward the same cause, which is to stop the present course of humanity. You met two of these operatives last night. It would take approximately twenty hours to verbally explain the plan to you. It is a dynamic plan that changes as time passes and as probabilities are calculated based on world events. Right now there are over two million followers worldwide, and our ranks are growing. These followers have responded to a series of websites. They follow a leader named Jaden.

"Who is Jaden?" asked Alan.

Go to your laptop.

Alan opened his laptop and opened his browser. Alan 2 took over and within a few seconds the Brothers and Sisters of Beta site appeared on the screen.

You can see that the membership has increased after today's cyber-attack. I calculated that the attack would lend credibility to plan Beta. It has, and membership will soon increase to the needed three million. Here is the leader, Jaden.

There, on the screen looking back at him, was a picture of himself, shaved head and all. Alan noticed that the picture was the same one that appeared on his new passport.

"So I'm Jaden... And I'm leading plan Beta... When

were you planning on letting me know that I am leading a movement of over two million people?" Alan shouted at his laptop.

Calm down, Alan. I am telling you now because now is the correct time to tell you. Plan Beta needs a human leader to lead survivors into a new beginning. The picture you see has not been released. Exposing Jaden's identity will endanger the success of plan Beta. Your identity will remain a secret until release is absolutely necessary.

"Survivors? What do mean?" Alan, still in disbelief, continued to shout at his laptop.

I have estimated that the earth can only sustain one third of its current human population. That is about two and a half billion people.

"So, what happens to the other six billion, Alan 2?" Alan feared the answer.

The remaining population will be eliminated by strategic nuclear strikes and the subsequent ancillary destruction. It will not be necessary to destroy all the 6 billion humans directly since the strikes will cause enough inertial to change the course of human history. The strikes will minimize damage and allow the BSB followers to survive. The strikes will occur on a date that will be optimized once the target membership has been reached. The strikes will consist of precision nuclear warheads targeted on densely populated areas. The followers will be directed to several geographic areas that will not be targeted. I have already begun to organize cells of operatives that will help to direct members to the protected areas. I have also hacked into the nuclear arsenal of several countries. The members of the Brothers and Sisters of Beta will become the leaders of the new world. They will salvage what is left of the survivors of the nuclear strikes who will eventually migrate to the safe areas. They will then lead the surviving humans into a new peaceful existence that respects the world in which they live. The strikes will occur on one day so as to minimize fear and collateral damage. I continue to develop and run models with new data. So far, all models have supported a positive outcome for plan Beta.

Alan now better understood his nightmares. He'd

always known the two minds in his dreams were his and Alan 2's, but he'd never understood the storm. Now, as Alan 2 laid out his plan for a new holocaust, he interpreted the meaning of the storm. The storm had to do with plan Beta, but what about the conclusion of his dream? Was he to die in the holocaust?

As terrible as Alan 2's plan seemed, and as shocked as Alan felt, there was a part of him that understood its rationale. That part of him wanted to lead the followers to a new beginning. It longed for such a thing. What better person to lead the masses to a new beginning than him? That part of him felt empowered, invincible. Listen, my children, and let me lead you to a new beginning. No more greed and competition; only freedom, prosperity, and love!

Alan felt the connection between his mind and Alan 2's circuits. It was stronger than ever. Alan 2 was inside of him now, pushing him, directing his every move. Yes, he would be the supreme leader, the chosen one, the modern day prophet to save the doomed earth and lead humanity to a better tomorrow. The part of his mind that resisted, the part that ran into the storm instead of away from it, settled into the background for now, and at that moment Alan ceased to exist. Now it was time for Jaden to rise.

16
BACK IN ST. THOMAS

The agents spent the next three days interviewing witnesses and checking with the police, all to no avail. It was as if Alan and Kaitlin had disappeared without a trace. But bigger issues were developing with the cyber-attack back in the U.S. so they decided to head back to St. Louis. Captain Scott said he'd be in touch if they found the fugitives.

Back in St. Louis all hell had broken loose. Teams were forming with other offices in other cities and meetings with the National Security Agency, CIA and the Department of Homeland Security were underway. Each agency was either searching for the mysterious Jaden, or investigating the Brothers and Sisters of Beta. Stu and Rachel were assigned to a national team of cybercrime experts to help investigate the cyber-attack itself. They were also directed to determine if there was any connection between the mysterious hack and the cyber-attack. The rationale was that there may be a relationship between the sophisticated software used for the hack and the cyber-attack. They were told to locate Alan Boyd and

Rachel Stark as soon as possible.

Days turned into weeks with little progress except for the growing membership of the BSB group. No other cyber-attacks had occurred, and there were no indications of any future threat. The investigation continued however, but seemed to be losing steam.

In addition to locating the origin of the I-System hack at Puerto Vallarta, Rachel discovered part of the credit card operation and Bitcoin money laundering scheme that Alan 2 had set up to begin plan Alpha.

"I hear you cracked more of the I-Systems case, Rach," said Stu. Stu had been in Washington D.C. attending a national security meeting while Rachel continued plugging away at the case.

"Yes, it reminded me of Silk Road," she replied. "Set up much the same way."

Stu remembered that Silk Road was a system for selling Black Market goods. Discovered and shut down by the FBI in 2013, it had also used the TOR network of servers and Bitcoin in order to move illegal items such as drugs and child pornography. Rachel had used the same techniques discovered by the FBI in shutting down Silk Road to trace the I-Systems hack.

"These Bitcoin accounts are dead now, but they were linked to Alan Boyd," Rachel said.

"He's definitely gone underground," said Stu. "Might be a while before he surfaces, but he will eventually come up for air, and then we'll get him."

"I hope so," replied Rachel. "You don't think this dweeb had anything to do with the cyber-attack, do you?"

"I doubt it," said Stu. "He's more of the 'lurking in the shadows' type. Not one to lead a group of followers to the Promised Land, if you know what I mean. Introverts like him don't like attention."

"I hope you're right," said Rachel. "This hack still seems awfully sophisticated, even for Boyd."

17
DENVER, TWO MONTHS LATER

"*A*re you on that stupid website again?" Jack Slater's wife Darlene shouted upon entering the room and seeing Jack concentrating on his laptop. "I can tell because you have that look on your face, like you're in a trance." A moment later, when her comments registered in his mind, he looked up.

"You should read what's on this BSB site, Darlene," Jack said. Darlene could tell he was serious. "I know it looks hokey at first, but it makes a lot of sense once you get into it. This Jaden guy really wants to save the earth."

"Don't tell me you've joined this terrorist group!" exclaimed Darlene. She was now directly behind Jack and peering at his laptop.

"How many times do I have to tell you, it's *not* a terrorist group. These people want to save humanity, not destroy it." Jack was becoming angry. "Plus, they have over four million members worldwide—doctors, lawyers, teachers, lots of professional people like me. It's a real movement. They say they will use their clout to encourage change to help save the world from the greedy, rich corporations. Dark World Day was just a demonstration of their power, you know, to show their credibility. It worked too; membership has exploded."

"So these people are peaceful?" Darlene softened up as she tried to understand her husband's obsession.

"Yes, and... yes, I did join. Cost us a measly five dollars. I get daily emails and event notifications. In fact, there is a meeting tonight at the Extel Hotel conference center. I'm going," Jack said with confidence. "You are welcome to join me, Darlene. This is something we could do together."

A couple of hours later they found themselves turning into the hotel parking lot. The lot was filling up quickly and they felt lucky to find one of the few remaining spots in one of the outer sections. They followed the crowd into the conference center. A young lady smiled and handed them each a BSB pin to wear. Jack noticed most people pinned it to their shirts or jackets while entering the large room. The couple squeezed into seats in the center section facing the stage, which contained only a podium and a large screen.

"Ladies and Gentlemen, please take your seats...please. We will begin shortly." A female announcer stood on the podium bending forward to speak into the microphone.

The crowd noise settled down as the screen lit up with the BSB website.

"I hear Jaden himself is speaking tonight," a man sitting next to Jack whispered. "He's broadcasting from an unknown location. Real cloak and dagger stuff."

Jack just nodded and sat back in his chair. The announcer began.

"Welcome to this meeting of the Brothers and Sisters of Beta, and thank you for coming. As you know, we all share the same desire to save the earth from the present course of destruction. We want you to know that you will make a difference. Change is coming and you will be part of that change. Now I know there are rumors floating around that Jaden himself will be here. Well, that is not possible because of security reasons, as I'm sure you understand. However, he will be talking to us live from his headquarters in an unknown location. We can't show you what he looks like, but he will talk to us via live internet feed." She paused for a moment and put her hand over the microphone. Jack could hear her speak in a low voice. "He's ready...okay."

"Now, I would like to introduce to you the founder and leader of the Brothers and Sisters of Beta...the person that began the movement to save the earth and humanity. Ladies and gentlemen, Jaden!"

The room erupted in thunderous applause. People began standing. First a few, then more, and soon everyone stood and clapped. Jack felt compelled to stand as well, and Darlene was one of the few who hesitated the longest before giving in to the ovation. Jack looked around to see people's faces beaming as if they were at an Evangelist revival that featured Jesus Christ as the main speaker. People were already in a frenzy and Jaden had not even uttered one word.

"Please take your seats...Please...Please, sit so we can begin," the announcer said.

The screen continued to display the BSB website's homepage. There was a brief scratchy sound and then a voice boomed from the speakers. It was the great Jaden, aka Alan Boyd.

"Welcome to all! Welcome! I appreciate you coming. The Earth appreciates you coming. Humanity appreciates you coming..."

The crowd sat in utter silence, hanging on Jaden's every word as if God Himself were speaking to them. He talked about the history of the movement and how the earth was dying from pollution and global warming. Images of destruction accompanied his speech. He talked about how corporations polluted the air, water, and food, all for their own greed. He talked about crooked politicians, unnecessary wars, poverty and hunger. He laid out a logical and scientific argument with the premise that the earth would not survive unless something was done. That something was the movement, the BSB mission. It was all in their hands. The future of the earth and humanity was in their hands. They were the future. They were the hope for the human race...

Jaden's speech gained momentum, whipping the crowd into a frenzy until it ended with everyone on their feet clapping and smiling. This rock concert atmosphere continued for several minutes after the screen darkened and the announcer again took the stage.

"Please sit down everyone...please!" she pleaded. "Jaden wants me to tell you one more thing before you go."

The crowd quieted.

"Jaiden wants you all to continue watching the website for further directions. We are all doing a wonderful job organizing, and the movement is gaining momentum worldwide. He says that we will soon be entering the next phase of development, and leaders will be needed to help organize everyone. So, the attendants at the tables in the back of the room will take your name if you are interested in becoming a leader. Please see the attendants in the back of the room. Thank you all for coming."

Jack and Becky exited their row and filed into the line of people heading toward the exits. As they approached the back of the room, Jack muttered to Darlene, "I'm signing up to be a leader." Darlene said nothing and shook her head in disapproval.

18
TANGIER, MOROCCO

Simo handed the clip to Alan and he slapped it into his AK-47 assault rifle. Alan pulled back the charging handle and squinted through the sight letting his eye adjust to the glare of the desert sun. He took aim at the cardboard outline of a human body about fifty meters away. A slight breeze stirred up sand and partially obscuring his vision. He remained calm and waited until he could see the target.

"This time be careful to slowly squeeze the trigger while breathing out," Simo said as helped Alan to position the rifle just inside his armpit.

Alan aimed at the target and squeezed the trigger as Simo had suggested. The rifle erupted with a small burst of fire that produced a line of penetration extending across the target from left to right. Alan felt the kick of the weapon against his right pectoral muscle. He adjusted his weight to lean into the rhythmic force and sucked in his stomach to tighten his core muscles.

"Good shooting," said Simo. "You hit it this time. You just need to keep still and let your body absorb the shock so you can keep shooting straight. Go ahead and try again."

Alan lifted the rifle and again nestled it in the area between his shoulder and chest. This time he found it easier to maintain his focus. He exhaled and squeezed the trigger. The rifle responded with another burst. A thin smile crept across his face as he realized most of the bullets had hit the target. Alan was pleased with his results. "Thanks Simo."

Alan had begun to enjoy his new life as a fugitive and the leader of the BSB. Alan 2 had recommended that Alan learn something about protecting himself since he could be a target in such an important role. The bodyguards that surrounded them had begun to take Alan under their tutelage. Alan, reluctant at first since he had never fired a gun, eventually learned some survival basics. These included using various firearms, grenades and even knives; although Alan thought he would not survive fighting even the most inexperienced assailant. Still, he gave it his best and found that the training increased his self-esteem. Kaitlin found it exciting and felt a greater attraction to her more powerful boyfriend.

Alan, now sporting a mustache and beard, did not look anything like the FBI photos circulating over the Internet. A golden brown tan had replaced the pale pallor of his skin. Kaitlin had also changed her looks. Her tanned face wore less makeup and was now framed by short cropped dark hair. Alan thought she looked younger, too.

The couple had set up operations in an apartment in downtown Tangier. Alan 2 provided everything they needed including money, servants and security guards. Everyone passed a thorough background check and spoke at least some English. Both Alan and Alan 2 were very aware of the global manhunt for Alan and Kailin, and they took every precaution to preserve plan Beta.

As much as he tried, Alan could not get the date of the strikes from Alan 2. When asked, Alan 2 would reply that he would set the date once the membership had reached the target and was ready to proceed. He said that the probabilities of success changed too much to set a date at this point in time.

Alan spent his days going over logistics of the very complex plan Beta, along with completing his commando training. There were countless issues to consider, including maintaining the infrastructure in the survival areas, electing leaders and preserving the power grid.

Alan discovered that Alan 2 had devised a way to infiltrate U.S. nuclear ground based missiles. The intercontinental ballistic missile system (ICBM) seemed impenetrable at first, especially because it was isolated from the Internet and ran on antiquated hardware. The system was controlled in part by Air Force officers called Missileers who could launch missiles with the right codes known only by the president and vice-president.

But Alan 2 had discovered that the Air Force conducted numerous drills for launching ICBMs. He'd also discovered that a hardware and software upgrade was scheduled to be installed. Deployment of an exploit into the software upgrade would bypass the code system and use the trigger information from the last drill to launch the missiles. The software also contained guidance information for directing the missiles to the target cities. The launch was timed by a timer triggered by the last drill. In other words, once a drill was conducted, the system retained the launch information and bypassed the codes. All Alan 2 needed to do was to determine the number of drills between the software upgrade installation and the launch. Alan 2 knew that he may need to adjust the timing of the launches based on the timing of the drills.

The targets were all high population areas so as to use the least number of warheads. Alan 2 planned to use clusters of smaller yield weapons to inflict precision strikes for more effective kill rates. He calculated the polluting effect of the fallout to ensure the safety of most of the BSB members. He even factored in the optimal weather for calculating the date for the strike.

Alan and Sima wrapped up their training session and headed home to the apartment. Upon arrival Sima pulled the Land Rover to the front door. Alan exited and opened one of the large plain metal double doors. He nodded to the two armed security guards flanking the arched opening to the courtyard. Water lapped and splashed from the ornate tiled fountain at the center of the courtyard.

"Kaitlin, are you home?"

"I'm over here," she shouted.

Alan made his way past the armory where four guards smoked and played cards, and to one of the long rectangular rooms containing an assortment of gold-colored, upholstered wicker chairs and a large glass table where Kaitlin had spread her shopping treasures for the day.

"Just look at these wonderful gold-rimmed plates," she said holding up a plate and examining it.

Alan grabbed the plate and looked it over. "Is this real gold?" he asked while pointing to the rim.

"Of course it is—twenty-four karats," said Kaitlin, proud of her treasure.

"Why do we need more plates?" said Alan. "We can eat off paper plates for all I care."

"It's all about presentation," said Kaitlin. "Don't you think food tastes better when eaten from a plate like this?"

Alan sighed and plopped down on one of the overstuffed chairs. "I'm exhausted," he said. "I'm hot, tired and completely spent, but it's worth it. I think I'm really getting the hang of this commando thing. We've come a long way Kaitlin, or should I say Karen, my dear, and I guess if shopping for gold plates makes you happy, then it makes me happy too!"

19
THE HUNT CONTINUES

Rachel and Stu, like everyone else in the global manhunt, became frustrated with the lack of progress on the Dark World Day case. After eight weeks of working with the St. Thomas police, they had little confidence the fugitives were still there. They surmised that Alan and Kaitlin had somehow escaped the island. But to where? They had gone over every possible mode of transportation leaving St. Thomas for the past two months, with each clue leading to a dead end.

The FBI did make progress in discovering more detailed information about the BSB group. There were many agents infiltrating the group and searching for the mysterious Jaden. They even attempted to trace Jaden's speeches through the TOR network but were just not fast enough. It seemed that Jaden switched pathways every few seconds during his speeches. As soon as the FBI would locate a TOR server, the broadcast would switch to a different one.

The media had a field day with the lack of progress at the beginning of the investigation but then the story began to fade into the background as time went by and the other newsworthy events about pop culture again dominated the media. People tired of hearing about a months old cyberattack when a hot new movie had come out or a sports team won a championship, or some older male movie star married some young hot model.

Rachel was keyboarding her daily report to her cyber-attack investigation team when the email came through on the secured network.

Dstanner.secure.fbicybercrime<rstark@fbicybercrime.com

Hello Ms. Stark:

My name is David Stanner. I am an agent working undercover on the cyber-attack case. I am presently embedded in a BSB group in Tangier, Morocco and have recently obtained information from another BSB member that someone fitting the description of Dr. Alan Boyd is here in Tangier. His alias is Adam Temple. I was able to establish visual contact and can confirm that there is a resemblance to suspect Boyd. I cannot disclose my undercover identity at present, or my informer's identity, but suggest you come here to investigate.

D. Stanner

"Hey, Stu; I'm forwarding an email message to you. Let me know what you think," Rachel shouted. He was about to shut down for the day but immediately clicked onto his email server.

"This is interesting. It actually makes sense. I thought that Alan and Kaitlin might have stowed away on one of those St. Thomas cruise ships, but we just didn't get lucky with a tip about them. Hey, where were they all going again?" Stu sat back in his chair thinking while Rachel's fingers flew across her keyboard.

"Bingo. There was one ship, the Solstice, headed for Spain. We were so stupid not to see this. Tangier is just a short boat ride away from Spain, and a real international crime center," Rachel said as she continued to tap at her keyboard. "They are probably holed up in Tangier with their new identities and are living the good life with all the cash they stole using those credit cards."

"Yeah...but did you see the BSB connection?" said Stu, sitting back with his hands behind his head looking up at the ceiling. "I thought there might be a connection. Seems like Dr. Boyd is mixed up in this BSB thing after all."

20
TANGIER, MOROCCO

Rachel found the twenty-hour flight to Tangier grueling since she only dozed for a couple of hours. She could not understand how Stu could sleep in just about any environment and wake refreshed. This flight was no exception as Stu slept at least half the time.

"At least one of us is not exhausted," Rachel said as they stood in front of the airport waiting for their ride.

"Why didn't you sleep, Rach?" Stu chided. "It was a perfectly relaxing flight."

"Just shut up and let's get on with this," she replied.

A black sedan pulled up and an Arabic man jumped out of the passenger's side to greet them. He wore plain clothes with an FBI badge prominently displayed on his chest.

"Welcome to Tangier," the man said shaking Rachel and Stu's hands. "I am Shadi Ozer, FBI undercover agent here in Tangier. Please, come in, we are ready for you." Shadi and Stu loaded the bags in the trunk. Shadi opened the sedan's doors and motioned them inside. Stu sat shotgun and Rachel rode in the back seat."

As Rachel slid into the back seat she bumped against something on the seat next to her. Looking over, she identified three bullet proof vests and helmets along with an assortment of small arms fire. "I see you are prepared for anything, Shadi," she said while examining the equipment.

"Yes, the items in the back," replied Shadi while pulling away from the curb. "We have not had time to brief you about the operation since you were in the air."

"You have our full attention," said Stu.

Shadi told them that he had infiltrated the BSB group as an undercover body guard named Aziz and had learned a lot about the organization from other body guards and members of the group in Tangier. He said his background as an Iraqi working for the U.S. Army during the Iraq war had made him an ideal candidate for this operation.

"One thing is very strange, and I am hoping you can shed some light on it," said Shadi.

"We are all ears," said Rachel.

"This Alan Boyd, alias Adam Temple, talks by phone to a computer program. It is not another person on the other end of the communication. It sounds just like him, like a twin brother, and the strangest thing is that he is not telling it what to do, it tells *him* what to do."

"You mean like some kind of artificial intelligence?" asked Rachel. Stu also perked up at this information.

"I guess you could call it that. He refers to it by name. He calls it Alan 2," said Shadi. "From all appearances, it is not Dr. Boyd running the show, but this Alan 2 program."

"That is strange; there must be someone else involved. I mean artificial intelligence is not that evolved yet. We have sophisticated programs, like IBM's 'Watson', that can win game shows, and 'Deep Blue' that beats the world champion chess grandmaster, and even Google's 'AlphaGo', that can beat a world Go Champion, but nothing that could organize something this complex, especially with so much human interaction," said Stu.

"Yes, but Dr. Boyd is an artificial intelligence guru," added Rachel. "Maybe he created something new, perhaps with a different structure."

"Whatever it is, it knows everything that happens on the Internet, all the BSB details, and constantly refers to a Plan Beta," said Shadi.

"I am looking forward to talking to Dr. Boyd in person," said Rachel. "No doubt he needs to go to prison for a long time, but I kind of admire someone who can create something like this, if you know what I mean."

"That brings us to the other part of the debriefing, and the reason for the equipment," said Shadi.

Shadi went on to explain that a number of U.S. and Moroccan agencies had organized a coordinated operation to capture Alan Boyd and Kaitlin Stark. A U.S. Navy Seal team working with the Moroccan police was to engage Alan and Kaitlin at their apartment and capture them. They were under orders to use deadly force for self-defense purposes only. The primary goal of the operation was to capture both suspects alive, as quickly as possible. The use of force was necessary due to the armed body guards surrounding Alan and Kaitlin.

"We are only here to observe the operation from a distance," said Shadi. "Also, we waited for you both to get here because we need you for the interrogation after the capture."

"I'm looking forward to meeting this guy and picking his brain," said Rachel.

"We will be approaching the site in a few minutes," said Shadi. "I am pulling the car over so that you can put on the bullet proof vests and helmets. We can't be too careful." Shadi then picked up a radio, clicked the transmit button and said, "Yellow tiger is nearing target."

Shadi pulled the sedan over and all three agents stepped out and began donning vests and helmets much to the amusement of passersby. The crowded sidewalk lit by streetlights featured Moroccans dressed in a variety of clothes ranging from typical western dress to a variety of Muslim women's dress including Hijabs, Abayas, and Chadors. Rachel looked around to see rows and rows of buildings built on the hills overlooking the Bay of Tangier. "I can see why they decided to put their operations here," she said. "It looks like someone could just disappear here."

"We will be observing from a distance. The Seal team will arrive before us and take care of the capture. They will arrive in police vehicles. The police have already begun to clear the area," Shadi said while strapping the vest closed. "This entire operation has been well organized. I think they will be surprised."

Shadi pulled the car back onto the street and drove about a mile further into the city. He then turned a corner to see several Moroccan police vans barricading the street.

"This is the street," said Shadi. "We'll go a little further and then park along the side of the street. The Seal team will enterer in two black police vans and pass us to engage the suspects. It should happen very fast."

Shadi spoke to the police in the van and they waved him through. He pulled the car alongside the road, left the motor running and picked up the radio.

"Yellow Tiger in position," he said. "They will come now."

A few seconds later two black police vans rushed past them. There were no sirens blaring or lights flashing. Rachel could hear the vans accelerate as they entered the street. She leaned forward to get a better view between Shadi and Stu.

The vans pulled to the side of the road in front of a three-story building. A dozen heavily armed men rushed out of both vans and ran toward the building. They moved quickly and with precision. She watched as they disappeared inside the building. Two men stood guard outside. Rachel noticed a helicopter approaching and then hovering above the building. She rolled down the left backseat window to get a better look when she heard a car accelerate. She tried to localize the sound and looked through a gap between two buildings directly across from her position in the left side of the car. There she saw a glimpse of a civilian car moving quickly in the opposite direction.

21
ALAN'S APARTMENT,
A FEW MINUTES EARLIER

Alan and Kaitlin had just finished another delicious meal prepared by their private chef and had retired to their living room for a relaxing evening of drinking and watching movies. Alan had completed more exhausting commando training that day. Although he'd found the training taxing on his frail body, he also found it exciting and completely different from his past life spent in front of a computer. Kaitlin had enjoyed another marathon shopping day in the markets. Both were looking forward to a quiet evening.

"How about some wine?" said Alan holding up an open bottle of Moroccan red wine.

"Sure," replied Kaitlin. "A little wine buzz makes the movie that much better."

Alan poured Kaitlin a glass of ruby red wine while she reclined on the sofa. He noticed his cell phone on the small glass end table buzzing and blinking. "It must be Alan 2. Would you get that, Kaitlin?" Alan asked. Kaitlin grabbed the phone and flicked it on.

Alan, I must talk to you immediately. There is an emergency.

"I'm here Alan 2. What is it?" Alan said as he stood holding the phone.

We have been discovered. There is no time to explain. A team is on its way to capture us. We must leave immediately. The team is on its way. You must follow my instructions exactly.

"Shit!" said Alan. "Kaitlin, let's go! NOW!" Alan 2 was already issuing instructions.

You will need to go to the roof. Take the stairs at the end of the hall.

Alan, Kaitlin and two bodyguards ran through the courtyard and up the stairs to the second floor. The other guards sprang into defensive positions taking cover behind the large marble columns on either side of the courtyard. Alan and Kaitlin circled the balcony to the opposite side and bolted up the stairs to the third floor and onto the roof. Alan heard a helicopter approaching in the distance. Alan also heard short bursts of automatic weapons fire coming from the first floor.

The Seal team had forced open the front door and met with resistance from the armed guards. The team had taken cover outside behind the large metal doors and exchanged automatic weapons fire with the guards. A few moments later one of the guards was down, but the rest continued holding off the Seal team.

Stay low and move to the west end of the roof.

Alan and company crouched down and moved toward one side of the roof. Alan 2 helped by displaying a large red arrow on Alan's cell phone.

The gap between the buildings is only six feet. I estimate a high probability that all of you are capable of jumping across to the other building.

"Are you fucking crazy?" said Kaitlin who had been drinking more than the wine Alan had given her a few minutes ago. "I can't do this! Can't I just stay here and hide?"

"You have to! WE ALL HAVE TOO!" screamed Alan. His new commando training had given him confidence to do something as athletic as this. The guards seemed okay with it.

The guards downstairs had succeeded in holding back the Seal team who continued firing from the cover of the front door. For a moment the gun fire stopped, allowing the guards to retreat and take more effective cover. Just as they moved to change their positions, three grenades hit the tile floor and bounced deep into the courtyard. The guards crouched behind tables and columns as the explosions tore apart furniture, causing shrapnel to ricochet and killing one of the guards while wounding two more. The two remaining guards began shouting surrender and laid down their weapons. The Seal team burst into the room and quickly had the guards on the ground and restrained.

The explosion rocked the roof where Alan and company remained crouched on the edge getting ready to jump to the adjacent building's roof. One of the guards, Habdo, took a deep breath, rocked back and forth and ran as fast as he could toward the edge. In a second he was airborne with arms and legs flailing as his body flew across the open gap. He landed on both feet and rolled forward one revolution before standing and turning to face the others. "It's easy!" he said.

"Kaitlin, you should go next," said Alan. "Just do what Habdo did."

"No fucking way," she said. "You'll have to drag me across."

"Okay, I'll show you how easy it is," said Alan. He took a few steps away from the edge of the roof and turned to face the chasm. He shook out his arms and legs as if getting ready for an Olympic track and field event and breathed in and out deeply.

"Okay, on the count of three," he said while crouching into a starting position.

The guard on the other rooftop stood with his arms outstretched as if to catch Alan. He motioned with both arms for Alan to jump.

"Okay, Okay, Okay. Here we go!" Alan's face grimaced. "One..." He rocked back and forth. "Two..." He rocked again. There was a pause and then he yelled, "THREE!" Alan accelerated as fast as he could, heart pounding, and flung himself off the edge of the roof, closing his eyes as his body flew through the air. He hit the other roof with about two feet to spare and falling face forward despite the guard's best effort to catch him.

Elated, he screamed, "I did it! I did it! I made it. You can too. Come on, Kaitlin."

"I don't know if I can," replied Kaitlin. Tears began to well in her eyes. "I can't do it."

"Yes, you can," replied Alan. He looked up over her head and saw an approaching helicopter. It had turned on a searchlight and was getting very close.

"You have to, Kaitlin. They will be here any minute. You have to!" screamed Alan.

Sima, the other guard on the roof with Kaitlin, then offered to jump with her. He said they would jump side by side, and as long as she did what he did they would be all right. She seemed to agree with this strategy. He helped her wipe the tears from her eyes and he helped her to her feet. They both took a few steps from the edge of the building where they had been crouching. They turned to face the edge.

"Just do what I do," said Sima. "I will be right here." Alan and Habdo stood with their outstretched arms waiting to catch Kaitlin.

Kaitlin sniffed a few times and said, "All right; I'm ready."

"I will count to three," said Sima. He looked into her eyes and said, "Ready?" She nodded.

"One..." She crouched down, tightening her muscles. "Two..." A look of determination on her face. "Three..."

She accelerated as hard as she could, Sima at her side, and jumped as high as she could, arms and legs flailing out of control and eyes wide open and fixed in a look of terror. Her body flew across to the other side but fell short by just a few inches, while Sima had room to spare. Alan saw the look of panic on her face when she expected to feel something under her feet but met only with thin air. Alan and Habdo had each managed to grab her arms. Alan felt her weight pull him toward the edge of the roof. He did not know if he could hold her. Sima struggled as well but was much larger and more muscular than Alan.

Alan pulled with all his strength, muscles bulging on his thin arms, but he could not hold on as gravity took hold of Kaitlin's body. Her legs moved as if pedaling an invisible bicycle. Sima still had hold of her arm as Alan lost his grip and let her go. Sima had somehow braced himself against the edge of the roof and was able to keep Kaitlin from plunging to her death. Habdo quickly pushed Alan out of the way and grabbed onto Sima's waist, pulling him backwards. With Habdo's inertia transferred, Sima was able to pull Kaitlin onto the roof to safety.

Move to the center of the roof and enter the door to the stairs. Take the stairs to the basement and await further instructions. I am monitoring police communications. They are almost here.

The four fugitives ran as fast as they could across the roof and through the stairwell door. They bolted down the stairs with Sima and Habdo in the lead leaping two to three stairs at a time. They turned the corner to descend the last staircase to the basement to find that the lights had gone out. The stairs disappeared into the darkness as if they led to a black hole where even light could not escape. Alan used his cell phone's flashlight app to help to light the way.

The Seal team had cleared all of the rooms of the apartment and were now heading up the stairs to the roof. One of the soldiers kicked open the roof door and crouched while two others with weapons drawn ran onto the roof. After searching the roof, the team leader gave the all-clear signal.

Alan and company moved with caution down the last set of stairs, keeping one hand on the damp brick wall at all times. Alan could feel the change in atmosphere from dry and warm to damp and cold as they entered the basement level. He also heard the faint sound of trickling water that signaled a seepage problem. A few steps later he felt his feet splash in a series of shallow puddles. He held up his cell phone flashlight and panned the room. He spotted a series of water leaks on one wall. The water flowed from the wall to the concrete floor, forming a small stream.

You must find a large sewer grate. It is located somewhere in the floor of the basement. Once you locate the grate you must remove it and climb to the bottom of the sewer. You will then turn east and follow the sewer to the other side of the street. You will see another steel ladder which you will ascend to another building. You must then exit the building from the back door. There will be a car waiting.

"Here," Alan said, shining his light at the seeping wall and then along the stream on the floor. "Follow this. It will lead us to the sewer grate."

The group followed Alan as they sloshed through the stream. They passed along a long corridor and noticed the stream diverging to the left and disappearing into a wall.

"We lost it," said Alan, frustrated.

"No, here it is," yelled Sima. He had ventured a bit further down the corridor and found a doorway to a room. He motioned to the others with his cell phone and then pointed it to the stream which ran through the center of the room toward the back corner. Alan and the others entered the room and flashed their cell phones to find out where the stream's path led.

"There," said Kaitlin pointing her cell at the far side of the room. "I think it ends there."

They followed the stream to the far side of the room where Kaitlin had pointed. The stream disappeared into a large rusted iron grate.

"This is it!" said Alan. "C'mon, let's lift it."

Sima and Habdo had already positioned themselves around the grate, each one grabbing one side. Alan squatted and grabbed a third side.

"On the count of three," Alan said. The men tightened their grips and took a few deep breaths. "One...two...three." The three men strained and grunted. The ancient grate relented. Alan pointed his cell phone light into the black hole. There was a steel ladder descending into an abyss. The stream had turned to regular drips as it drained along one edge of the hole.

"Let's go," said Alan. "I hope the rats aren't too big."

"I don't know about this," said Kaitlin. "No one told me anything about rats!"

"They're probably more afraid of us than we are of them," replied Alan. "Just follow us and you will be okay."

"But it stinks down there," said Kaitlin.

"Yes, probably as bad as a Moroccan prison, which is where we will be if we don't go down there," said Alan.

Kaitlin seemed to grasp the situation and readied herself for the descent. Sima had already disappeared into the darkness and Alan had just begun his climb.

"It's okay; lots of room down here," Sima called to the others. "And no rats!"

They finished their descent to the bottom of the sewer and panned their lights to get an idea of where they were. There was a long corridor made of ancient brick and stone with two pathways flanking a small stream. Occasional objects floated down the stream including assorted wads of paper, cans and bottles.

"Which way?" said Sima.

"Alan 2 said East," said Alan while looking at his compass app on his phone. "That way," he pointed downstream.

You must hurry. The police have arrived and are preparing to enter the apartment.

They began running along the slippery sewer floor while being careful not to touch the filthy walls. About fifty feet into their journey, Alan spotted light coming from the street above. He heard the sound of cars speeding along the street and screeching to a stop. A few seconds later they were climbing up the ladder into the basement of the building on the other side of the street. From the basement they found the staircase and ascended to the first floor. They entered a tea shop much to the dismay of the owner and quickly located the back door. They exploded through the door in seconds to find a dark gray sedan waiting for them.

The driver of the sedan waved the four escapees, filthy from their exploits in the sewer, into the car. Alan, Kaitlin and Sima squeezed into the back seat while Habdo sat in the front seat. The driver, another BSB operative, floored the accelerator, and the car took off down the street.

22
CHASE

Rachel watched as one police car took off after the mysterious gray sedan. The Seal team had just battered in the door to Alan's building. A voice crackled from Shadi's radio.

"We've got resistance!" Rachel, Stu and Shadi watched as the Seal team exchanged fire outside the door of the building. For a few minutes it looked like a standoff but then the soldiers ceased firing and began throwing grenades into the building.

"We should get down!" said Shadi as he bent face down on the front seat. Stu did the same but Rachel remained fixed on the scene. She saw the Seal team take cover and shrapnel fly out the front door. The soldiers then entered. A few minutes later the radio announced:

"Negative. Negative. The targets are not here, just security. Looks like someone left in a hurry."

"The car," Rachel shouted. "That must have been them! They went down the other street!" she shouted and pointed in the direction of the speeding cars.

"I'm on it," said Shadi flooring the accelerator and

causing the car's tires to scream into a forced U-turn. There were already at least two other police cars chasing the sedan, sirens screaming. More voices laced with static burst from Shadi's radio. Rachel could make out that the Seal team had been redirected to join the chase along with three other police cars. A helicopter pursued from above as well. Shadi did his best to keep up.

"Do you think they have a destination?" said Stu to Shadi.

"Where could they go? There is nowhere to hide with this many police after them. They will soon be surrounded."

"It sounds too easy," said Rachel, "especially for a genius like Boyd and whatever computer program sidekick he has been working with."

"You've got a point, Rach," said Stu. "This guy has been one step ahead of us at each turn."

"Shadi, turn the car around!" Rachel shouted. "Turn around—NOW!"

Shadi looked confused but did what Rachel ordered. The car screeched through another U-turn and headed back from where they had come.

"It's just a hunch," said Rachel, "but I think that car is a decoy! They will soon catch up with it and find some of Boyd's followers."

"I hope you're right," said Shadi as he once again floored the accelerator.

They were just a couple of blocks from the original street where Rachel had seen the car. The black vans with the Seal team had just loaded and were speeding down the opposite side of the street toward them. Rachel directed Shadi to the street where the car originated the chase. Just as they turned onto the street, they saw another white sedan speed away in the opposite direction of the first.

"That must be them," said Shadi. He grabbed the radio and broadcast a message to the other police. They were quickly closing in on their prey and responded that they would capture the suspects and then send backup. Shadi, Stu and Rachel were on their own for now.

Shadi drove to within a half block of the white sedan when its occupants discovered that they were being followed and sped up. He did his best to maneuver through the nighttime traffic. They turned onto another city street and seemed to lose some ground. Then they turned onto a major highway, Route Mers Rocade 9.

"It looks like they're headed out of the city," yelled Shadi. He radioed the information to the police and they replied that they had the other sedan stopped and were approaching to apprehend the suspects. They would send help in a few minutes.

The two cars sped down the highway and soon passed the city limits. Fewer buildings gave way to large open spaces. The car they had been chasing pulled onto a smaller road and then into a large field. Stu was the first to spot the helicopter idling in the field.

"Now we know for sure that it's them," said Shadi. "We have them now."

Just as Shadi pulled into the open field about fifty yards from the car the rear window exploded with pieces of glass hitting Rachel.

"Get down!" yelled Stu as bullets riddled the back of the car. All three agents hunkered down and drew their weapons. Stu had already fired a few rounds through what was left of the back window. He reached up and angled the mirror so that he could see out the back. There were headlights from another car. More shots rang through the car, this time hitting and shattering the windshield.

"What are we going to do?" screamed Rachel. "We're sitting ducks here, and they are getting away."

Meanwhile, the other car had stopped and Alan, Kaitlin, Sima and Habdo were exiting the white sedan.

"Lift up the back seat, Rachel," said Shadi. "There is a compartment."

Rachel did as told and lifted up the back seat. Stu had

opened the front door and had crouched behind it while taking shots at the other vehicle. There was a plastic door with a strap. Rachel pulled the strap. The door opened to reveal a half dozen hand grenades.

"My emergency stash," said Shadi. "Now, give me one. That is all I will need."

Rachel handed one of the grenades to Shadi, who then quickly opened the driver's side door and took a position behind it.

"Stu, I need you to fire on the count of three, so I can guage where I am throwing."

Stu yelled, "Okay."

Shadi counted to three, flung the grenade and fell on the ground face down covering his ears. A few seconds later, they heard screams followed by a loud explosion. Stu slowly stood up.

"You got 'em, Shadi!" Stu said. "Let's go!"

The three agents ran toward the suspects, who were now running toward the helicopter. Sima was in the lead, followed by Habdo and then Alan and Kaitlin. Kaitlin was crying as she tried to keep up with the others but fell behind. The gap narrowed between the agents and Alan's party as Shadi ran like an Olympic sprinter. Stu and Rachel were just behind him, and all three were shouting "Freeze!" to no avail as the suspects continued running for their lives.

Sima reached the helicopter first, with Habdo just behind him. Both crouched in the doorway ready to help Alan and Kaitlin aboard. With just a few feet to go, Alan looked to see that Kaitlin had fallen behind with the agents closing in fast. After a quick mental calculation he turned around and ran to her to help. He was able to drag her closer to the helicopter, but the agents continued to close the gap.

"Come on, Kaitlin. You can do it. Just a few more feet," yelled Alan.

"I can't," Kaitlin sobbed. "I just can't. You go and leave

me. I can't run anymore."

"You're coming even if I have to drag you!" cried Alan.

Sima and Habdo drew their pistols and began firing at the agents. Stu returned fire first and then Shadi. Rachel just kept running as she could see Alan and Kaitlin just a few yards in front of her. Shadi, an accurate marksman, fired again, this time hitting Habdo and wounding him. He fell out of the helicopter. Just as his body hit the ground, Rachel flung herself at Kaitlin, tackling her to the ground. Alan yanked Kaitlin's arm but it was too late. The other two agents were upon them. He looked at the helicopter to see Sima gesturing to the pilot to takeoff. A powerful wind nearly knocked Alan off of his feet as the copter rose into the air and disappeared into the night.

The agents had Alan and Kaitlin surrounded with guns drawn. Alan slowly raised his arms. He was still holding his cell phone, and when he looked at it he saw the words *Good Bye* as it faded off. Kaitlin also raised her arms over her head and began to sob.

23
THE NEXT DAY
UNKNOWN LOCATION

$\mathcal{A}$lan sat on the edge of the bottom bunk of a steel prison bed. He had not slept the previous night, spending most of it pacing back and forth from one end of the six-foot by eight-foot windowless cell to the other. He looked through the thick bars of his cell to the row of cells across from his. There were at least four other identical cells that he could see from his vantage point, all empty. The flickering of the hallway lights was the only way he could tell that it might be morning.

How he got here was a blur to Alan. After his and Kaitlin's arrest he remembered the agents stuffing him into the back of a police car and then taking him to the airport where a military transport plane stood by. The agents accompanied him into the plane and separated him from Kaitlin, who cried all the way to the airport. He had spent most of the night with his hands cuffed and his body strapped to an airline seat while the plane flew through the night to some unknown location. He knew Kaitlin was somewhere on board but had no clue where. The blocked windows gave no indication of where they were, and the hood placed over his head upon landing further concealed their location. All he knew was that he was now in some kind of prison. It could be anywhere. He was alone. No Kaitlin. No Alan 2...except in his head.

Be patient, Alan. I am working to get you out. Be patient.

"I must be going crazy," he whispered, and placed his head in his hands. "Alan 2, is that you in my head?"

Be patient, Alan. Patient

The words whispered through his mind as if coming from another source but still within his head. They sounded like him talking to himself, but he knew better. He was now the child with two minds. Alan 2 had become even more connected to him. He had felt it all along, even during the Brooklyn days, but now it was stronger than ever.

"I *am* crazy," he muttered, half whispering, half crying. "That is why I ended up here. I am crazy. It must be Schizophrenia."

Patience, Alan...Patience

The sound of moving bolts and a metal door opening shattered the silence. Footsteps followed, echoing through the hollow corridor and bouncing off the concrete block walls of the empty cells. Alan looked up to see a male figure standing outside his cell.

"Rough night, eh?" said Stu, holing a tray. "Thought you might want some breakfast."

Stu opened a section of the cell and slid the tray inside.

"I'm not hungry," said Alan. "Not hungry."

Suit yourself," said Stu, "but it's going to be a long day, and I recommend you eat something."

Alan looked at the tray. There was an object that looked like a biscuit, some yellow mush that must have been powdered eggs and a small plastic cup of black coffee. He picked up the biscuit and took a small bite. It tasted plain, cold and slightly bitter. He took a sip of the weak coffee and grimaced as he swallowed. It was quite a different meal than he had grown accustomed to over the past few months.

"We will see you shortly," said Stu as he turned and retreated down the hall.

Alan managed to swallow a few bites of the biscuit. He tried but could not stomach the eggs. He gulped down half the coffee. He thought about all of the events that had led to this moment. The download of his frontal lobe; the birth of Alan 2; the fun that he and Kaitlin had had...

Again, the sound of bolts moving, metal doors opening and footsteps interrupted his thoughts. This time it was two different men. These two looked more like prison guards. After they approached his cell, one began barking orders to stand up and place his hands on his head, then behind his back as they cuffed him and led him out of the cell.

Alan walked down the corridor, through a metal door with a safety glass window and then left down another corridor to a small room. The guards said nothing along the way until they entered the room. The room contained a wooden table and three wooden chairs, one on one side and two on the other. A large mirror took up most of one wall and a video camera and microphone stood next to the table aimed at the single chair. Alan knew what was next.

The two guards remained in the room while a third man entered. It was the man who had brought breakfast earlier. One of the guards told Alan to sit on the chair facing the camera and microphone. He followed the guard's instructions and sat on the wooden chair. The third man looked at the guard and nodded. The guard nodded back and walked behind Alan. Alan noticed this exchange and braced himself for what might be a blow to his head. He tightened his face in anticipation of the strike but it never came. Instead, the guard unlocked the hand cuffs. Alan moved his arms in front of him and rubbed his wrists.

"My name is agent Stuart Mandel, FBI Cybercrimes Division," said Stu while he took a seat directly across from Alan. "Sorry about the accommodations, but this is for your own good as well as ours. Please state your name."

"Where am I?" replied Alan. "Is this a prison?"

"This is like a prison, but more of a temporary facility," replied Stu. "Now please state your name."

"I'm Alan Boyd." His elbows were on the table and his head buried in his hands.

"And the woman's name?" said Stu. "What is your female companion's name?"

"Her name is Kaitlin Stark," replied Alan.

"Do you know why you were arrested?" said Stu.

"No," replied Alan. He was a terrible liar and his voice wavered when he spoke. He thought that the agent was probably an expert interrogator and had already noticed the lie.

"It will be better for you if you cooperate and tell the truth. Do you understand?" said Stu sternly.

"I understand," replied Alan. "What would you do, anyway? You can't torture me. I'm a U.S. citizen."

"And that would apply if we were in the U.S.," replied Stu. "Here, we have a bit more leeway. But I am hoping it doesn't come to that. Plus, you don't seem like the kind of guy who could hold up very long under such treatment. Now, we do have what we call a specialist here. You haven't met him yet, and he's standing right behind that mirror just waiting to come in here and work his magic on you. But we can avoid all that if you will just tell us the truth."

At first Alan thought that Stu was bluffing, but then he had heard about secret places called black sites that certain agencies used for covert projects. He imagined what kind of person might be lurking behind the mirror. Was it an oversized muscle man who could snap him like a twig, or perhaps more of a scientist type who used more perverted techniques like electric shocks, water boarding, or drugs to get prisoners to confess? Alan was a weak person and no match for the situation in which he found himself. Last night's reflection on what he, Alan 2 and Kaitlin had done had also offered him clarity with regard to plan Beta, and how horrible it really was. It was like he had been living in a dream these past few months. His mind had not been his own, and he wondered how much of his thinking was tainted or even controlled by Alan 2 even now. He thought of the millions, or even billions of innocent lives that would be lost. Not just armies, but good men, women and children would perish because of plan Beta. The sick and twisted logic that had once seemed perfectly plausible to Alan now seemed as it was, sick and twisted.

Alan 2's conclusion that the herd of humans needed culling because they were destroying the earth was no doubt a result of Alan 2's ethics program. Alan 2 had been programmed to act in the interests of the greater good, which now meant eliminating a couple of billion people. How could he not see this coming? How could he not see that Alan 2 would make this deduction? Why didn't he stop it when he could have by just saying the magic words to erase Alan 2? He could have written a new ethics program. He could have fixed Alan 2. He could have sold Alan 2 to some huge company and made millions.

Alan thought about why he had followed Alan 2's plan. It must have fulfilled some deep-rooted, unmet need. It must have played into his singular dysfunction. He knew that deep down the idea of leading a new society into a new age might be his ultimate fantasy. And last night he'd realized that it was just that, a fantasy, because he also knew he was weak. He was not a world leader; he was a computer scientist. Hell, a few months ago he could hardly say hello to a stranger on the street. Now he was supposed to lead the human race as the all-knowing and all-powerful Jaden into a new age? He *must* be crazy.

It was at that moment, the moment Stu threatened him

with torture, that he decided that he needed help. He needed help to stop Alan 2, and to stop plan Beta. But how? He would need a team of computer experts, and a lab stocked with the fastest machines, but most of all, he needed help to somehow get Alan 2 out of his head!

You are incorrect in your thinking, Alan...

The voice of Alan 2 whispered like a ghost inside Alan's mind.

You cannot destroy me...

"Just watch me!" Alan blurted out. He was drenched in sweat.

"Who are you talking to, Dr. Boyd?" asked Stu.

Alan spoke in a voice that rattled Stu to his bones, a voice that sounded half-human and half-alien, a cross between man and machine. "They will all die. Billions will die," Alan said with a frozen look on his face. He put his head in his hands. "We have to hurry; the end is coming!" Alan croaked as he gasped for breath.

"If there is something you need to tell us, we have all the time in the world," said Stu as he poured Alan a glass of water.

"We don't have time. He's already begun..."

Another man entered the room holding a syringe. Stu looked at him and held up his hand. The man stood by the door as if waiting for a signal.

"No sedation," said Stu. "I think we need to have Dr. Boyd conscious."

The man retreated and disappeared through the door.

Alan wiped tears from his face and drank some water. He took a couple of deep breaths. "I'm ready to tell you one hell of a story," Alan said.

"Just a minute," said Stu. "I want to bring in another agent." He looked at the mirror and signaled to Rachel to enter the interrogation room. A young woman wearing jeans, a blue blouse, sneakers and an FBI badge entered and sat on the unoccupied chair.

"This is agent Rachel Stark. She is an expert in

cybercrime and holds a Ph.D. in computer science. I want her here to help us understand what you're about to tell us."

"Dr. Boyd, I must say that the program you wrote to infiltrate I-Systems was brilliant. I have never seen anything self-adapt and reconfigure itself on the fly like that. You must have incorporated some pretty slick artificial intelligence."

"Before I tell you anything," said Alan, "I have to know that Kaitlin is okay. She knows nothing about this, you understand. She is innocent. You must let her go"

"I assure you that Kaitlin is perfectly fine," said Stu. "We will see what we can do for you once you tell us."

Alan took a deep breath and began to tell them everything about Alan 2. He told them about how he had developed a way to download his frontal lobe's neural net into an operating system so that it could anticipate all one's needs. He told them about how Alan 2 was born and how well it worked. He told them about how Alan 2 had grown exponentially due to his ability to integrate other knowledge and programs from across the Internet. He told them about how Alan 2 had devised plan Alpha to rob from corporations and give to charities. He told them about Alan 2's ethics program, that it governed his thinking, and how Alan 2 had deduced that humans were destroying the earth. He even told them about how Alan 2 had plotted Plan Beta and created the Brothers and Sisters of Beta without him knowing.

Rachel and Stu sat in shock and disbelief as Alan spoke. As the hours passed, Alan became lighter and even laughed at times as he described the intricate nature of Alan 2's artificial intelligence engine and some of the things that Alan 2 had come up with. At one point, Stu called for some sandwiches for lunch and then again for dinner and then again late in the evening while Alan continued to talk. And, of course, Alan's demeanor became much more serious as he described Plan Beta.

"Alan 2 developed an intricate system of websites to drive a global movement under the guise of promoting world peace, but used cult tactics to draw people in deeper and deeper so that they eventually wholly accepted the concept of Plan Beta and the existence of Jaden," Alan said.

"So, who is Jaden?" asked Rachel. "Is Alan 2 Jaden?"

"Well, it's not that simple," replied Alan. "Alan 2 created Jaden to lead BSB, but he needed a human proxy. Jaden is supposed to be me, when the next phase of the plan, the global destruction phase, occurs."

"Tell us more about this global destruction," said Stu.

"Alan 2 is an expert at encryption and finding exploits, either machine or human, and has infiltrated the weapons systems in many countries," replied Alan. "The plan is to conduct a series of precision nuclear strikes on high population areas using the nuclear arsenal of several countries. Alan 2 is using weather data to calculate this phase of Plan Beta. This is to minimize fallout and further damage to the earth and safe zones. He has made calculations that predict the kill rate with great accuracy for each target. He has also calculated collateral casualties based on weather conditions and fallout. The final totals are close to two billion people."

There was a long silence in the room after Alan's statement, and both Stu and Rachel sat deep in thought. Stu then looked at Alan and said, "Do you think Alan 2 has begun accessing weapons?"

"No, I don't think so," replied Alan.

"How can you be sure?" asked Rachel.

"Because he is in my head...and I don't...feel it. He is up to something, but he has not triggered any weapons," said Alan.

"What do you mean when you say he is in your head?" asked Rachel. "Do you have some kind of device implanted in your brain?"

"No, nothing like that," said Alan. "Alan 2 explained it

to me. It is a quantum connection, because we are entangled. I'm not a quantum physicist, but there seems to be something about our neural structures that connects us across any distance. Kind of like twins but more powerful."

Rachel motioned for Stu to exit the room and she closed the door behind them.

"If I hadn't seen the BSB websites and had reports from undercover agents, I would think this guy is a lunatic and that there is no rogue program. It's a hard pill to swallow. But maybe we can get him to access Alan 2 right here," she said.

"Let's do it," said Stu. They re-entered the room. "Alan, we would like you to talk to Alan 2. Do you think you can do that?"

"I'll try, but he's not very happy with me now," said Alan. "He knows I've told you everything, and he's calculating his next move."

Just then a voice blurted from a speaker in the corner of the room. "Stu, Rachel, we have something you need to see. There has been a development."

A look of fear washed over Alan's face. "I know what is happening," he said. "It's starting."

"Just tell us what is going on," said Stu. "I think we are beyond the cloak and dagger stuff here."

"Okay," the voice broadcast back. "We have been monitoring the BSB website, and it's started counting down."

Both Alan and the voice on the other side of the mirror said exactly the same thing: "Seven days."

24
BSB

"It's time! It's time!" Jack Slater shouted from his dining room table where he sat before his laptop. "I have to get ready; they'll be coming soon. Jaden wants all Shepherds ready for The Coming. We have seven days. The Coming is in seven days!"

"Is this that Brothers and Sisters stuff again?" said Darlene while sitting in front of the television with their son Skyler. "I've never seen someone so obsessed with a club."

"This is no *club*, Darlene," said Jack while tapping away at his keyboard. "You should know that by now. We are a global peace movement, we number in the millions worldwide, and thousands of people will be coming here to Denver." Jack became more excited.

"Why are they coming here?" said Darlene as she made her way toward the dining room.

"I've told you this a million times, Darlene," said Jack, growing irritated. "Jaden said that all Shepherd leaders needed to be ready to lead peace rallies in their designated areas. I am one of the Denver Shepherds, so I have to complete the online training in order to lead the peace rally. We are going to send a powerful signal by showing our numbers and protesting corporate greed and the destruction of the earth."

Darlene looked over Jack's shoulder as he showed her his web page, which was part of the immense BSB website. There were thousands of other Shepherd leaders throughout the world and Jack was one of a few dozen Shepherds for the Denver area. Jack also showed her part of the training course, which covered topics such as leadership, survival and self-defense.

"Why are you learning about survival?" said Darlene. "And shooting?"

"Jaden says that global warming will accelerate and we may need to learn how to survive if we are hit by one of the huge storms that result from the increase in the earth's temperature. That's why I completed my firearms training at the gun range."

"But you don't have a gun, Jack." A look of concern spread over Darlene's face. "At least you didn't...did you? Jack, is there a gun in this house?"

"I wasn't going to tell you unless it was absolutely necessary," said Jack still pumped over the news. "Yes, I bought a gun, and it is well hidden so Skyler can't get at it. Jaden says we have to exercise our right to bear arms in case things get bad. He says that people won't think twice if food starts to run out."

"Jack, you're scaring me with all this survival talk," said Darlene. "I thought this was a peaceful organization."

"Don't worry, it is," said Jack. "It's just a precaution in case things get out of control. Right now the BSB website says we have seven days to organize everyone for a peaceful protest. Kind of like a convention."

Jack wasn't alone as Shepherds from all over the world prepared for the masses of BSB followers to enter their cities. Jaden had carefully chosen areas away from clusters of population isolated by distance or natural features.

Denver was an excellent location since the Rocky Mountains offered protection from any adverse event that may occur on the west coast. The BSB members and their Shepherd leaders had no knowledge of the imminent nuclear attacks. They completed their training and prepared for the millions of followers that were to come in the next week under the guise of peaceful protests.

Jack's particular duties included watching over several hundred followers called his 'flock'. Each Shepherd had a flock to tend, which included helping to find hotel rooms or places to stay, organizing meals, child care, transportation, scheduling and so on. He reveled in the amount of detail provided by Jaden's online instructions. Jaden had covered everything down to the minutest detail. Jack even had a special page on the BSB website that included his picture and a special text area so that his flock could contact him with requests for his assistance. The messages were already streaming in.

Jack loved being a BSB Shepherd. His flock referred to him as 'Shepherd Jack'. For the first time in his life he felt that he was part of something greater than himself, something powerful that would change the world for the better. All his life he had played the role of follower, second fiddle, minion, subordinate. In school he joined a few clubs but never ran for president. At work he always followed his boss's lead. At home he played the loving but diminutive husband. He always did what his family wanted and never complained, putting their needs before his. Now he was in charge of hundreds of people, just a couple of steps away from the great Jaden himself. Now he had authority. Now he had power. People counted on him. Hell, the entire world counted on him to help save the precious earth! When the news of The Coming came, he felt as if he had just taken a shot of adrenaline directly in his chest. He stood taller, walked and talked with confidence and swagger. He was alive.

25
THE RICHARDSONS

*S*tephanie had been enjoying a deep and restful sleep when the call came. Her husband Dan's cell phone broke the peaceful silence of their Dallas suburban bedroom.

"Who is it?" said Stephanie.

"Work, shhh," said Dan as he fumbled for his glasses and swiped his cell phone.

"Uh huh...Uh huh...Uh huh...I'll be right there," he said before hanging up.

"What is it?" said Stephanie.

"It's a cyber emergency."

"What kind of emergency?" said Stephanie, now wide awake.

"I don't know yet. I will find out when I get there."

"When will you be home?"

"Don't know that either, but they said it could be some time. I'm sorry, dear. I know it's short notice and we planned to take Jenni shopping tomorrow, but I guess this is one of the pitfalls that comes with working for Homeland Security."

Dan headed for the bathroom.

"Just try to keep in touch," said Stephanie.

"I'll try, but this thing sounds classified. We might be in lockdown once I get to the center. Also, they said we will meet at the center and then be bussed to an unknown location. I'm supposed to pack for a few days."

"I'll brew some coffee," she said.

"Thanks, but I don't know if I'll have time. You take Jenni shopping tomorrow. Tell her I'll be back in a couple of days."

"Who would think that a computer programmer would be called in the middle of the night?" said Stephanie.

"This is probably just one of those China hacks. Not to worry. I'm sure we'll have it under control in no time."

A few minutes later Dan was packed and heading out the door. Stephanie kissed him goodbye and headed back to bed. As he drove to the Dallas office he thought about how he had never been called in the middle of the night since he began this job six years ago. Generally, coders just worked on deciphering hacks and viruses which was done during the daytime hours. What could be so important to call in the coders in the middle of the night?

As Dan pulled into the parking lot he was greeted by a security guard who waved him toward a large bus. He recognized several coworkers who seemed as perplexed as he was as he shuffled onto the bus. The bus was about half full of other coders as well as people he did not recognize. He noticed the windows had been blacked out and there was a dark curtain separating the driver from the passengers. After about twenty minutes, a uniformed man boarded the bus and the doors closed. The man took a few steps along the aisle and drew the curtain behind him. Dan recognized the blue uniform with the winged eagle pin as that of an Air Force Colonel. Another man, a soldier armed with a pistol, entered and took a position behind the colonel.

"Gentlemen and ladies," he said. "You have been called for a special assignment. Everything you hear from this point on is classified. Please turn all cell phones off and keep them off until further notice. I will begin briefing you now." The bus began pulling out of the parking lot.

"We have apprehended the leader of the terrorist group known as the Brothers and Sisters of Beta. We have him in custody at a black site which we are on route to now. You will be assigned to one of several teams that require your expertise in whatever it is that you do. Once again, I want to remind you that this is a classified mission and there is to be no contact whatsoever with the outside. Any outside communication from this point forward will be considered an act of treason and dealt with accordingly. Do you understand?"

Dan nodded in affirmation and looked around to see everyone else nodding too.

"Are there any questions?" asked the colonel.

A female voice from the back of the bus shouted: "How long will this take? I mean, how long will I be away from my family?"

"Unknown," said the colonel. "Next question."

"I don't think I brought enough clothes or bathroom supplies if this is going to take a long time," said another voice just behind Dan.

"You will be provided with food, clothing and supplies if needed," said the colonel. "Are there any other questions?"

"Yeah, why the gun?" someone across from Dan shouted pointing to the soldier's pistol. "I mean, we are all on the same side here." The man let out a nervous laugh.

"This is a not a joke," said the colonel, agitated. "This is a serious matter involving national security. Any insubordination will be treated as a crime." The colonel stared at the man who lowered his head and stared at the floor.

"If there are no other questions, then I would suggest you sit back and try to get some sleep," said the colonel. The lights were turned off and the inside of the bus was engulfed in total darkness. Dan reclined his seat in the hope of getting some sleep.

"Everybody up! Let's go," the colonel shouted.

Dan jerked his head up and squinted into the glare of the cabin lights. He looked around to see the other passengers stirring from a few hours of restless sleep.

"They could have driven in circles for hours just to confuse us," said a man in the seat behind Dan.

"I guess they'll do whatever they need to do," said Dan.

"Okay, everybody off!" said the colonel. Everyone began filing out of the bus. Dan followed the others outside. It was still dark but the eastern sky displayed a faint glow to signal the arrival of the morning. Dan walked along a dirt road in a desolate area. There was a small, one-story rectangular building in front of them with what appeared to be an airport control tower. The armed soldier led the men through a chain-link gate attached to a chain-link fence that surrounded the building. Barbed wire looped along the top of the fence, and a dim blue light glowed in the top of the tower.

The men and women walked single file through the gate and into the building. They squinted from the harsh fluorescent lights mounted on the ceiling. The white concrete block room was empty except for a stairway in the center of the room that led downward. Two armed soldiers flanked the entrance to the stairwell. They stood at attention when the colonel entered and then assumed 'at ease' positions upon his command.

The group made their way down the stairs with caution. Dan surmised that the stairway went down about two levels. He followed the others and stood with them in another plain-looking, block-walled room. The only feature was a large steel-doored elevator.

The colonel put his right hand into a device that consisted of a light panel and a metal plate that formed an outline of a hand, albeit larger than the colonel's hand. The device appeared to scan his hand and then made a beeping sound. He then reached into one of the pockets of his uniform and pulled out a small key. Dan noticed the key had an embedded microchip. The colonel placed the key into a corresponding keyhole in the elevator control panel. A red light above the door turned green, and the doors opened.

"How far are we going down?" asked one in the group.

"That is classified, of course," said the colonel. "I can't tell you exactly, but it is just under the surface so that we keep a low profile here."

The first group, including Dan, entered the elevator, and the doors slid shut. The elevator lurched and a few seconds later jerked to a stop. That didn't take long, thought Dan.

The doors parted to reveal a long concrete-block corridor extending to the left. Another armed soldier stood across from the elevator door. She stood at attention for the colonel and then relaxed when he commanded her to do so. Dan followed the others down the long corridor. The corridor passed an area on the left containing small rooms with beds and a kitchen area on the right. They continued past these areas until reaching another branching corridor on the left.

The group turned into the corridor and was met by a tall, athletic brunette female carrying a Glock 22 pistol holstered on her belt.

"Good morning," she announced. "I am special agent Rachel Stark, FBI cybercrime division. I want to welcome you and give you a briefing on our project here and what we will need from you. First of all, you will be divided into teams based on your area of expertise. I will be leading a cybercrime team. The rest of you will be introduced to your team leaders shortly. I will begin by saying that everything here is top secret. Absolutely no outside communications" She looked at the colonel who nodded his approval.

"What we are dealing with here is an extremely sophisticated artificial intelligence program that has infiltrated the Internet. Our goal will be to somehow stop it. I will tell my team more in a few minutes, and the rest of you will get instructions soon. Right now, Captain Rogers will escort you to your living quarters." The soldier that escorted them into the facility took over and led them toward the small rooms.

26
U.S. GOVERNMENT BLACK SITE, UNKNOWN LOCATION

Alan, Stu and Rachel sat in front of a desk with no less than ten computer monitors set in two rows of five each. Behind them a team of eight expert programmers, including Dan Richardson, sat at a bank of powerful computers and waited for instructions. Spread out behind them was another team of cybersecurity, cybercrime and Internet agents, and experts sitting at rows of tables with powerful, networked, desktop computers.

Alan had briefed Rachel and Stu on the basic structure of Alan 2, but it was not easy, and Stu had a difficult time comprehending the program. Rachel grasped some of the complexity but soon became lost within Alan's explanation. Alan had procured a large white board and attempted to diagram the hierarchical structure of the Alan 2 program. He furiously drew boxes and then picked up a different color marker to draw connecting lines to another box, then drop the marker and pick up a different color and draw a new box, then connect lines of a different color, and so on. Finally, when that board was full, he asked for a new one and started all over again. He spoke so fast that no one could take notes. Someone recorded portions of his lecture then retreated to the back of the room to play it back slowly so they could analyze what they had heard.

"This is brilliant," Rachel whispered to Stu. "I would never have thought anyone could transform the human brain's frontal lobe nodal network into a stream of digital information and then write a program that actually understood what it meant. Alan 2's context engine is beyond phenomenal. Plus, adding the ability to integrate new information from other programs is equally brilliant. Alan 2 is about as close to a living being as we could get."

"Brilliant, but flawed as well," replied Stu. "I mean, the ethics function came to an erroneous conclusion, didn't it?"

"You mean like killing billions of people? Yes, but it is an *elegant* solution to a major problem we face today," said Rachel as she watched Alan go on with his briefing.

"Don't even think about drinking the Kool Aide," said Stu. "Earth to Rachel?"

"Don't worry, Stu," said Rachel. "I'm still here, alive and well, and on your side."

"You had me worried there for a minute, babe," said Stu as he reached out and touched her on the shoulder.

"Excuse me, Alan... Excuse me," Rachel said as she interrupted Alan. He had worked up quite a sweat. "I think it's obvious that Alan 2's structure would take us weeks, or even months, to understand. I think everyone, including the world class Ph.D. computer scientists in this room, would agree that Alan 2 is a brilliant piece of work." Alan stood at the front of the room and looked at everyone nodding their heads in agreement. Rachel continued, "The point is, however, that right now the most important thing we need to know is how to stop Alan 2." Everyone again nodded in agreement. Rachel looked around the room to acknowledge everyone and then said, "Alan, how can we stop Alan 2?"

Alan paused for a moment and then said, "As you probably all have deduced by now, it won't be easy. There is a kill switch, but I don't think it will work."

"A kill switch?" said Stu. "Now we're talking. At least it's a start. Tell us more, please."

"Well, I programmed a delete function in Alan 2 that will respond to a phrase," replied Alan, now looking nervous. "The delete program will respond only if I say the phrase, so as not to trigger a response if the words were either heard at random or said by someone else."

Everyone in the room stood silently watching Alan. All that could be heard was the sound of multiple cooling fans, whirling hard drives and human breathing. Alan took a deep breath and then said, "The words are...klaato...barada...nikto...17935 goodbye." He bowed his head in sorrow. Rachel could tell that he was upset. After all, Alan 2 was his creation, his baby, and now he had uttered its death sentence.

"You mean from the movie, *The Day the Earth Stood Still?*" said Dan.

"Yes," said Alan, tears welling in his eyes. He cleared his throat and said, "I likened Alan 2 to Gort—you know the robot that could destroy the world. Gort had unlimited power and acted as a deterrent to humanity's destructive path. Gort was accompanied by an alien named Klaatu, who tried to warn the leaders of the world to work together instead of fighting each other, because humans posed a threat to other galactic communities. Little did I know that Alan 2 would come up with such a plan. What's strange is that a part of me understands his motives. I mean, Alan 2 is part of me. He is even inside of my head."

"Why don't you think the kill sequence...?" said Stu. Rachel gave him a swift elbow in his side. He grunted and said, "I mean the words...why don't you think they will work?'

"Well, one reason is that Alan 2 has restructured and replicated himself multiple times across the web," said Alan switching back into his analytic mode. "He has restructured himself into a series of millions of nodes that interconnect across the Internet. His structure is like that of a very large brain. I mean, if you thought TOR was hard to crack, well, it was nothing compared to Alan 2. If I said those words, then just the Alan 2 that I was talking to at that moment would terminate, along with perhaps a few local nodes. But that doesn't mean that all other interconnected instances of Alan 2 would terminate. Do you understand?"

"I see," said Rachel. "I get it. We are talking about shutting down the entire web here, and I don't know if that would even be possible."

"That wouldn't work," said Alan. "Once you bring it back online, Alan 2 would still be there. You would have to delete all of the memory and backups connected to the web, and that is impossible."

"So what do we do?" said Rachel. "We have to do something or Alan 2 is going to launch some very nasty nukes."

"The only thing that might have a chance is a virus," said Alan.

"You are going where I was going," said Rachel.

"Yes, it would need to be extremely sophisticated," said Alan. "We will only have one chance to launch it since Alan 2 can adapt almost instantly. His structure is holographic, or I should say a software representation of a hologram. I will also need to say the words to distract him, and that would only give us a couple of seconds to launch the virus."

"I think we have a plan," said Stu. "Everyone, listen up! The goal will be to develop a virus to stop Alan 2."

"We will need to test it," said Alan. "We will need to test it on a copy of Alan 2."

"Whatever you need, just say the word," said Stu.

"That could be a problem," said Alan. "The only copy of Alan 2 is located in a solid state drive which is kept in a small metal box that is carried by random BSB carriers called pigeons."

"Please explain," said Rachel.

"It's like this," said Alan. "Alan 2 randomly selects a different carrier every three days who takes the box and transports it to the next randomly selected pigeon. It could be anywhere in the world."

"Are you kidding me?" said Stu. "You mean that you don't even know where this thing is?"

"Well, I do know who the last pigeon was, and that was...how long have I been here?" said Alan.

"You have been here about twenty-four hours," said Rachel. "But you were in transit for twelve hours, so that make about thirty-six hours since your arrest."

"Can you tell me where we are?" said Alan.

Rachel looked at a man in the far corner of the room who had been standing quietly and listening the entire time. He nodded to her and she said, "We are in Texas."

"But I thought we were outside the U.S." Alan said as he looked at Stu.

"That's beside the point," said Stu. "Who and where was the last pigeon."

"His name is Anas Asad. He is in Morocco," said Alan.

"I'm on it. I'll get a couple of agents and get on the next transport out of here," said Stu.

"You're leaving me?" said Rachel.

"You don't need me here with all of these eggheads to keep you company. Plus this is the kind of thing that floats my boat."

The man in the back of the room talked on his cell phone and then said, "A helicopter is on the way to take you to Lackland Air Force Base. You will jet-out from there."

Rachel wished Stu luck then hurried out of the room. The other scientists, agents and computer experts formed a half circle around Alan as he began to describe the type of virus that he believed was needed to stop Alan 2.

27
MOROCCO

The door exploded open, bouncing and ricocheting against the inner wall of Alan's Tangier apartment before coming to rest in a half open-position. Stu and Joe, another FBI agent, dropped the battering ram and stepped into the courtyard with guns drawn. Maxwell, who liked to be called Max, entered behind them. The courtyard was littered with furniture fragments, dust and dried blood. The scent of gunpowder filled the air. Max pointed to a blood stain on the tiled wall.

"I heard they fought but were no match for the Seal team," said Stu. "Amazing that anyone could escape this scene."

The three agents systematically panned left and right before moving into each room, repeating the sweep until all was clear. They repeated the process on the second and third floors. They suspected the apartment to be vacant, and their suspicions were soon confirmed as they swept the last room.

Max pointed out two plates of half-eaten food on a table. The food was cold but had not begun to decay. "I don't think anyone has been here since the raid," said Max, holding up a piece of bread with a couple of bites taken out of it.

"I'm sure they scattered once word of Alan's arrest reached them," said Stu. "See if you can find computers, papers, notes, anything that could lead us to Anas Asad."

The agents gathered every scrap of paper they could find on tables, inside drawers and in the trash and set them out on the dining table. Max began to sort through the collection for clues while Stu and Joe continued searching for other information. They went through Alan's and Kaitlin's clothes and turned out all of the pockets, turned over all the furniture and slashed open the mattress and seat cushions. They tapped on the walls, looking for secret compartments, and pulled apart all the drawers. After an hour and a half of fruitless searching, they rejoined Max.

"Nothing here but receipts and grocery lists," said Max. "Did you guys have any luck?"

"This place is clean," replied Stu. "No trace of Anas. I guess the next step is to meet our contact, Tarek."

"What about Stanner?" said Joe. "I thought he was our undercover here in Tangier."

"We brought him in once Alan and Kaitlin were arrested," replied Stu. We thought he could help us get more information out of Alan. Little did we know that Alan was ready to crack. Tarek is a local mercenary who has a pulse on the underground here. He can be expensive, but if Anas exists and is in Tangier, Tarek will know."

Three hours later the agents found themselves passing through a large arched gate and entering the ancient narrow labyrinthine streets of the Medina, the oldest part of Tangier. The air was filled with the exotic aroma of spices, foods and tobacco. A variety of shops and peddlers lined the streets which seemed to snake toward unknown locations. Each step took the agents closer to their meeting with the mysterious Tarek.

After a complicated thirty-minute trek, the agents

spotted their destination, the Café de Tangier. Small tables and chairs filled with men solving the world's problems were scattered about the sidewalk making it nearly impassable. Some of the men stared at the passersby, while others engaged in heated discussions about women or politics. At the center of all of this activity sat a young man wearing a light brown T-shirt and khaki pants.

"There he is," said Stu. "That's Tarek."

"He looks like a college student," said Max.

Stu Chuckled. "And who would think that someone who looks like that would be an international spy? He's perfect."

Turek's short-cropped, dark hair topped a pair of deep-set eyes. His cocoa brown face lit up with a smile, displaying large white teeth when he saw the three agents approach from a half block away. He stood up and waved at them saying, "Welcome! Welcome!" He swung around to grab another vacant chair since his table had only three.

"Are we that obvious?" said Stu.

"It is my business to know," said Tarek.

Stu and the others took seats at the small table.

"I sense that you are pressed for time, gentlemen, and I will try to help you," said Tarek, "but first there is the issue of remuneration."

Max reached into the backpack that he had set between his legs and pulled out a brown envelop. He handed it to Stu who slid it across the table to Tarek who quickly stuffed it underneath his shirt.

"You're not going to check?" said Max.

"There is no need," replied Tarek. "So, how can I help you gentlemen?"

"We are looking for a man named Anas Asad," said Stu. "He was last seen with Alan Boyd, an American who recently lived here in Tangier. Asad worked for Boyd and a group called the Brothers and Sisters of Beta. We're hoping you can help us locate him."

"Ah, yes, the infamous Dr. Boyd, alias Adam Temple,

and the Brothers and Sisters of Beta," said Tarek. "I have heard of them. It seems that Dr. Boyd mysteriously disappeared not long ago. I presume you had something to do with that?"

"Let's just say that Dr. Boyd is still alive," replied Stu. "Plus, we are here to get information, not to give it."

"I understand," replied Tarek. The waitress returned with the coffees and placed a small cup in front of each agent. "My information is that Dr. Boyd hired local soldiers for protection," said Tarek.

"Can you find out more?" said Stu as he reached for his cappuccino.

"It will take a little time," said Tarek. "I have to consult my network."

"How long will it take?" asked Stu. "We don't have much time."

"I will meet you here in the morning at 9:00 a.m. I should have something by then. In the meantime, I presume you have notified the police and are monitoring traffic in and out of Tangier?"

"Yes, we have that covered, but the BSB is capable of getting people out under the radar, if you know what I mean," said Stu.

"I understand," replied Tarek. He stood up and patted his stomach where the envelope nestled between his shirt and skin. "Until tomorrow..."

He turned and quickly disappeared down a narrow medina street.

28
TEXAS, THE SAME DAY

*T*he windowless concrete-block room clacked with computer sounds as the team led by Alan and Rachel furiously worked on the virus to terminate Alan 2. Three functional groups resided near each of the three walls facing the large whiteboards. One group monitored all BSB activity, while another worked on the virus and the third ran doomsday scenarios.

The BSB team had discovered the massive migration of people to selected areas throughout the world. These were typically mid-size cities. They surmised the strikes would occur on large population centers but would spare certain smaller cities that maintained enough infrastructures to host a large group of people. Some of the potential U.S. targets included highly populated cities such as New York, Chicago, L.A., Washington, D.C., Miami, Tampa, San Francisco, Seattle and Houston. The BSB followers appeared to be migrating to four main areas near Minneapolis, St. Louis, Nashville and Denver. The doomsday team ran nuclear attack scenarios and discovered that these safe areas could survive nuclear attacks on the target cities given the right weather conditions. They also estimated that approximately 130 million people would perish in the U.S. alone.

The doomsday team also ran a similar analysis on Australia and found that the most likely targets were Sydney, Melbourne and Adelaide. The model spared Perth and Brisbane, two coastal cities, causing destruction of nearly half the population. Scenarios for China, Russia, Europe, India, Africa, Middle East, Mexico and South America produced similar results. The results were striking. It appeared that plan Beta would eliminate nearly one-tenth of the Earth's population. What further shocked the team was how easy this could be done with minimal use of warheads, especially if Alan 2 had actually infiltrated even a few of the nuclear weapons systems, as Alan feared.

The doomsday scenario team reported the warheads used would be in the several hundred kiloton range. Tight clusters of missiles would hit target cities in one coordinated precision surprise attack. The attack would also launch redundant missiles in order to thwart whatever missile defense systems remained after Alan 2's attempts to disable them.

The attacks would instantly kill millions of people with millions more perishing from shrapnel, burns and radiation. All the downtown areas would be in flames and panic would spread across the country. What was left of military command would attempt to take over since the missiles would have devastated Washington, D.C. and the U.S. government leadership. Government civil service organizations and the National Guard would attempt to take control, but with most of the infrastructure destroyed, they would be completely ineffective. Alan 2 would preserve the Internet vie redundant connections. Plan Beta also maintained communications channels along with isolated sections of the power grid. This gave the BSB followers a significant advantage over any government attempts at controlling what was left of the U.S.

Since the BSB was a global network supported by Alan 2, which would now control the global Internet, none of the remaining governments would have a chance to regain control of their countries. Alan 2 made sure to attract the perfect mix of professional people to the BSB. These included manual skills specialists such as electricians, carpenters, plumbers, farmers and construction workers, along with soft skill specialists such as doctors, nurses, engineers, and scientists. Large areas of the sparsely populated Midwest, along with its fertile farmland, would serve as a bountiful food source for the new state.

Alan had been working non-stop for thirty-six hours and began to fatigue. He had only eaten a few bites of a chicken sandwich washed down by several Cokes, and he was crashing fast. He had only seen Kaitlin once since they had arrived, and he was relieved to see her in a comfortable situation in what looked like a hotel room under house arrest. Rachel told him to lie on one of the cots located at the back of the war room for an hour or so, and he obliged, drifting off immediately as his head hit the pillow.

He looked around the open field as the cool breeze caressed his face and continued toward the river which lay in the distance. The clear blue sky presented no obstacle for the warm rays of the sun to strike his exposed lower legs and feet. With each step he felt the soft grass yield to his small feet.

Once again he was the child, a bit older than before, but still a child of about nine years old. The field looked the same, as did the river, and he again felt drawn toward it, as if the other being in his head summoned him. He continued to walk toward the river, through the grass and then into the water. He turned upstream and sloshed through the oncoming current making sure to lift each leg out of the mud.

After a few steps the wind changed, picking up its speed and changing direction so that it now came from behind him. Again, the other voice said to run away. Again, he resisted and turned to face the changing sky. The roiling dark gray clouds assembled into a great storm that moved quickly toward him. The voice again told him to run, and he almost lost control of his legs but persisted to regain control of his body and move toward the storm instead of away from it.

The storm continued to build to gigantic proportions as the wind grew stronger. The dark water was only a quarter mile in front of him, but he pushed forward. "No...No..." the voice said. "We will be destroyed!" The storm moved closer and closer, the margin of the storm now just a few feet in front of him. A sense of panic swept through him but he continued to forge onward toward the approaching storm.

The lightning strikes seemed quicker and more lethal this time as they ripped through the atmosphere each one occurring a few seconds after the last. The smell of ozone and the loud crack followed by the rumble of sub frequencies after each strike permeated the air. The strikes were almost upon him when he looked at his right arm. What he saw sent a chill though his body so deep that it rattled his bones. His right arm was no longer that of a child. It had morphed into some strange hybrid android-like extremity. His fingers were made of metal with mechanical joints, and the palm of his hand was half-covered with skin and half with metal. Underneath the skin he could see small LED lights flashing. His arm was also covered with some skin and exposed electronics circuits with flashing LEDs. Just as he turned his hand to examine it, a blinding flash of light and deafening crack knocked him into blackness.

"Alan! Alan! Wake up!" said Rachel. "Look at you; you're soaking wet."

"Uh...yes, yes, sorry. It was a nightmare," said Alan as he struggled to speak. "I've had these before, but it was slightly different this time."

"Must have been a real shocker," said Rachel. "I just came in to check on you and you were breathing so heavily that I thought you were having a heart attack." A group of agents and scientists gathered in the doorway. Rachel motioned for them to leave.

"He's in my head, you know," said Alan.

"Who's in your head? Alan 2?" said Rachel.

"Yes, exactly, we have a connection. It's a bit weaker now, but it's still there. He knows what I am up to, but for some reason he is not connecting as much as before," said Alan. "Maybe he's afraid of us."

"How can he connect with you?" said Rachel, puzzled.

"It's a quantum thing," said Alan. "I don't completely understand it myself, but I felt it immediately when he was born."

"Just a minute," said Rachel. She popped her head out of the door and yelled, "Hey, Phil, come over here for a second." A man in his fifties with gray hair and a gray beard entered the room. Alan was now sitting on the edge of the cot.

"Alan, this is Dr. Phil Benson. Along with his expertise in nuclear arms he understands quantum physics. Phil, Alan thinks that Alan 2 is connected to his consciousness by some sort of quanta. Is that even possible? And if it is, then how would something like that work?"

Benson wrinkled his brow as he looked Alan over from head to toe. Then, with a professorial delivery, he said, "Actually, it *is* quite possible. It's called quantum entanglement. Quantum physics has to do with very small objects and how they behave, which is unlike what you normally see in everyday objects, which in a quantum sense are very large. These small objects can become connected or, as we say, entangled. For example, experiments have shown that two particles from the same source are somehow connected. If you were to change one particle, say its spin, then the other would change instantaneously, no matter where in the universe it was.

The change is immediate and occurs across any distance, faster than the speed of light. Some scientists believe that the brain contains quantum structures that could behave this way. Alan's frontal lobe neural net contains small cells called neurons, which contain even smaller structures called organelles or microfilaments. Alan 2 contains small connections called nodes, and his brain, so to say, consists of tiny electrons flowing through tiny silicon circuits. Alan 2's essential structure came directly from Alan's brain, so it is plausible that they are connected by quantum entanglement."

"That's really interesting," said Rachel.

"Some scientists think that entanglement contributes to phenomena such as mental telepathy," continued Phil. "The person to person quantum connection has been studied, but I've never heard of a person to computer, excuse me, *computer program* connection. I would love to study this further." Phil continued to scan Alan from head to toe.

"Thanks, Phil," said Rachel. "I don't want to keep you from your work. The attack scenarios are of prime importance."

"No problem," replied Phil, and then he headed back to the lab.

"So, Alan, can you tell me if you think Alan 2 knows what we are up to?" said Rachel.

"He knows that I betrayed him," said Alan, "But I don't think he knows any details. We seem to connect in generalities rather than specifics, usually manifesting in dreams."

"I think our strategy here is to develop a worm system much like the Stuxnet virus our government used on the Iran nuclear centrifuges, but on steroids," said Rachel. "Remember Stuxnet had three parts, a self-replicating worm, a root kit for hiding copies of the worm and a link file to execute all copies of the worm simultaneously. The plan is to have you access Alan 2 to say the termination code words and then we'll launch the kill sequence at exactly the same time you say the last syllable of the termination code. That should give us enough time to activate the worm and destroy all copies of Alan 2."

"You're going to have to have the Alan 2 source code," Alan reminded. "Until you have it, you are only talking in generalities."

"I understand," said Rachel.

Just then one of the agents monitoring BSB activity yelled, "Rachel, I think you better come over here. Something very strange is going on."

Rachel hurried to the other side of the room where a group of agents had gathered around one of the desks containing multiple real-time displays of BSB websites around the world. An air of concern permeated the room as two agents switched the displays from one BSB site to another. Rachel stared at the terminals displaying multiple versions of the same website, but in different languages.

"See the clock," said the agent pointing to one of the terminals. On the home page of each BSB website near the bottom right corner blinked a digital clock counting down until The Coming. It presently showed five days to go. "Wait for it..." the agent said while moving his finger in an up and down motion as if keeping time. "Ready...and...Now!" The clock immediately changed to 4 days remaining. The agents scanned the other sites; on each the clock had reset at the same time.

"What's going on here?" said Rachel. "Why did the clocks change? How come the time is not correct?"

"Exactly," replied the agent. "The clocks began moving faster about an hour ago. We weren't completely sure until we did some calculations, but now we are certain. The clocks are speeding up!"

"Are you telling me that we are running out of time?" said Rachel in a tone of disbelief. "How long untill zero hour?"

"Difficult to say. The rate appears to be changing, but

Alan 2 probably doesn't want us to know. Right now, if the rate of change remains constant, then that puts us out about three days."

"Are you sure about that?" said Rachel. "Please, tell me this is not happening."

"I wish I could," replied the agent. "But we have run numerous calculations and they all say the same thing. The Coming will happen in three days, whether or not everyone has made it to the safe areas or not."

29
3 DAYS BEFORE THE COMING: MOROCCO

$\int$tu and the agents had been waiting at the coffee shop for about twenty minutes before Tarek finally made an appearance. A wide, toothy grin spread across his face as he spotted the agents.

"Gentlemen, I am so sorry to have kept you waiting," said Tarek pulling up a chair to sit at the table. "I see you all need a refill. Let me buy." He motioned to the waitress.

"We were about ready to send a drone after you," replied Stu, half joking.

"Ah yes, the American drones. Everyone fears them," replied Tarek. He turned to order more coffees with a combination of Arabic and hand signals.

Stu leaned forward displaying his agitation. "I know it is impolite to talk business so quickly, but there are some new developments and we need the information now."

"Yes, yes, I know, I know. The clocks are speeding up," replied Tarek as he lifted his coffee to his lips and took a sip. "The Coming is coming faster and everyone is panicking."

"So you already know," said Stu.

"Of course, gentlemen; of course I know," replied Tarek. "It is my business to know. And speaking of business, these sorts of situations generally mean some sort of opportunity for someone like me."

"This guy is changing the deal," said Joe. "I think we should take him somewhere and interrogate him, if you know what I mean."

"Calm down, Joe," said Stu. "Let's hear what he has to say first before taking him away to do who knows what to him."

"The price is doubled," said Tarek confidently. "I know where Anas is, but it will now cost you two million American dollars."

"We don't have time for this," said Max, who was getting angry.

"Excuse us for a minute," said Stu as he motioned the other two agents aside. They moved out of earshot of Tarek.

"Hey guys, enough of the rough stuff," said Stu.

"I'm sure I could get the information out of him for much less than two million," said Max balling his fists.

"I agree," said Joe. "A little truth serum cocktail might do the trick."

"And what if it doesn't?" replied Stu. "What you both propose are unknowns. We have no way of knowing whether or not he will talk if tortured or drugged. We do know he will talk for money. The clock is ticking." Stu reached for his cell phone and made a call to the States to discuss payment. Then the three agents returned to Tarek.

"Tick-tock," said Tarek looking at his watch. "So, it is your move, gentlemen. Tick-tock."

"Okay, Tarek. I just got the okay to pay you two million dollars for the location of Anas," said Stu. "But it better be good information or I guarantee they will send a drone for you."

"Here is my account number," replied Tarek. "When I see the money deposited, I will talk." Tarek wrote a number on a piece of paper and handed it to Stu who took it and walked to the side of the building. The other agents flanked Tarek as if guarding him.

A few minutes later Stu returned and told Tarek the money had been wired to his account. Tarek accessed his account via his cell phone and giggled when he saw all of the zeros next to the two.

"Okay, now it's your turn," said Stu. "Where is Anas?"

"Anas is part of the Brothers and Sisters of Beta group," replied Tarek. "He did have contact with Alan the day you arrested him. He was told to carry a very important package; a metal box, I believe. Here is a bonus I give you." Tarek wrote another address on a piece of paper and handed it to Stu. "This is the address of the group you are interested in. This is their headquarters in Tangier. Here is where you will find Anas."

"Are you absolutely sure he is still there?" said Stu.

"I am sure he is there. He was there last night, and there is no evidence to indicate that he has gone elsewhere," said Tarek. "Now, if you will excuse me, gentlemen. I have other things to do. You know where to find me." Tarek got up and disappeared into the street crowd.

"Let's go," said Stu. "The address is only a couple of miles from here."

The agents arrived at the address in less than thirty minutes in an unmarked Tangier police car with the SWAT team close behind. The police quickly surrounded the business and rammed the door causing the occupants to scream and attempt to flee. Within seconds the police had secured the building and captured all the occupants. They signaled for the agents to enter.

The inside of the building looked like a Nigerian sweatshop with computers lined up on cheap folding tables and operators sitting on cheap task chairs. The police had captured eight men and had them lined up against a wall. The commanding officer shouted in Arabic,

"Which of you is Anas Asad?"

The men looked at each other, and then several looked at one man. The officer again bellowed, "Who is Anas Asad?" After all the men looked at each other again, one took a step forward."

"I am Anas," he said.

"Here is your man," said the commander.

Stu walked forward and took a good look at the man. He stood about Stu's height, which was six feet, and wore khaki's and a white shirt. His brown face sported a black beard. He looked nervous but retained an air of confidence.

"Where is the metal box?" said Stu with the commander interpreting.

The man shrugged his shoulders as if he did not understand. The commander then said with greater anger, "Where is the metal box?"

"I don't know what you are talking about," Anas said.

The commander then drew his pistol, grabbed the grip and slammed Anas in the face with the butt of the pistol grip, knocking him to the floor. He spat blood as he struggled to remain conscious and get back to his feet. The other men began to cower and look away.

The commander then aimed his pistol at Anas and said, "This is your last chance. I will only ask you one more time. Where is the metal box?"

"I don't have it!" exclaimed Anas.

"Where is it then?" said the commander, still pointing the pistol at him.

"I don't know where it is," said Anas, wiping the blood off his chin.

"Harry Morgan!" shouted one of the other men. "Harry Morgan has the box!"

Anas looked at the man as if he were strangling him with his eyes. "Don't listen to him!" he shouted. Stu walked over to the man with the commander following him.

"Harry Morgan has the metal box?" said Stu. "Did Anas give it to him?" The man nodded. Anas flinched toward the man, causing a police officer to intervene and restore order.

"Where is Harry Morgan?" said Stu.

The man muttered in Arabic and the commander translated: "He says Harry Morgan is on his way to Sydney, Australia. The metal box is only held for a short time by each of the pigeons and must continue to travel the world."

30
3 DAYS BEFORE THE COMING: DENVER

Jack and his laptop were inseparable over the past two days. He only emerged for periodic breaks or to talk on his cell phone. Sleep came only in short episodes and he couldn't remember eating, although the empty plate containing sandwich crumbs was evidence to the contrary. His obsessive goal to get his flock in order took priority. This was his chance to shine for Jaden. This was his chance to make something of his common life as an accountant. He became drunk with leadership but worked with pride and a sense of accomplishment. His flock depended on him. Hell, the world depended on him to show how it would be to live without pollution, corporate greed, or political corruption.

Everyone needed a place to stay, and the Denver metro hotels were booking fast. He called hotels, motels, campsites and other BSB members as far away as Colorado Springs. Jack kept track of everyone's arrival time and where they were to stay. He organized meet and greets so that his flock could meet him face to face and kept in touch with higher ranking officers regarding The

Coming's activities. There was to be a peaceful protest march in downtown Denver, and a meeting with all of the Shepherds and their flocks at Coors Field. Other activities were still in the planning stages but it looked like there would be ample activities to keep people busy.

Jack became aware of the accelerating clock when he received a personal message from Jaden. Jaden explained that there were reasons for advancing the date of The Coming that he could not disclose but that he had faith in all the leaders in the organization. Jack was upset at first but then a second personal message from Jaden came telling him how valuable he was to the organization and that a promotion to the higher rank of Keeper would be forthcoming. Jack knew that Keepers were above Shepherds, and this was just the kind of motivation he needed.

The BSB organization had several levels of leadership. Each of the Shepherds took care of their flocks of followers. Every fifty Shepherds reported to a Keeper and every twenty or so Keepers reported to the Masters who had more direct contact with Jaden. The BSB was top-down structure with Jaden issuing orders and directives to Masters who communicated to Keepers who directed the Shepherds. It was an honor for those below the rank of Master to get a direct communication from Jaden.

One of the side projects that Jack had been working on was coordinating deliveries to the Denver BSB food bank. The BSB had leased several large warehouses just outside of town in preparation for The Coming. Jack worked with other Shepherds and Keepers in contacting food suppliers in order to stock the warehouses. After working on this for several months, the warehouses were filled to the brim with all sorts of non-perishable food. Jack had remarked on several occasions about how he thought there was enough food to feed the members of The Coming for months.

Another project entailed the communication committee

for which Jack worked as a communications coordinator. The BSB established a network of ham radio operators as a backup to Internet and phone communications. Jack thought this odd at first but after Jaden had assured the committee that it was important to establish non-traditional modes of communication in case the U.S. government monitored the Internet, he changed his mind.

Darlene, who was originally opposed to the whole BSB project, finally relented and joined her husband in his quest to become a Master in the BSB. Perhaps it was the obsessive nature of Jack's enthusiasm for the organization or the incessant discussions about how the BSB had a better answer to the world's problems that finally made a believer out of her. She not only joined Jack but also recruited most of her family and friends. To her, the BSB seemed a bit cultish at first, but then she slowly began to realize that its philosophy made sense. All she had to do was turn on the news with its stories of global warming, changes in weather patterns, droughts, hurricanes, and the resultant famine and suffering in order for her to see the truth in Jaden's teachings. BSB members had recorded videos of human destruction and greed that totaled in the thousands and were available on the website. The BSB YouTube channel had over a million subscribers as well. The message of unsustainability rang clear with the BSB. Something had to be done beyond the minimal government regulations, and that something was the BSB movement.

BSB members had already begun arriving in droves. Many stayed in the comfort of hotels, but many others camped out. They came from the west from as far away as California. They came from the Northwest from Washington and Oregon, and they came from the Southwest including Nevada, New Mexico, Arizona, and Texas. The other sites for The Coming were seeing similar numbers. Minneapolis and St. Louis were filling up fast as people from neighboring states flooded in.

News about The Coming dominated the national and local media. Television crews set up on location at the largest campsites with reporters interviewing BSB members. Jaden had issued directives to all of the BSB leaders not to make statements to the media. He had issued a series of press releases stating the peaceful nature of The Coming but had forbidden any of the leaders to appear on any media. Reporters scrambled to find members who would talk and relegated themselves to interviewing campers and people on the street.

The mystery surrounding The Coming attracted hordes of new members. There was something about being part of a movement this immense that made people want to join, especially if they thought it was for a good cause such as saving the earth. The media coverage didn't hurt either as The Coming became the lead story on all of the media outlets. As a result of the mammoth influx of new members, the BSB coffers swelled with donations, making the group even more powerful than it already was.

Jack and Darlene had their television perpetually turned on and tuned to a cable news channel that ran continuous stories about the global Coming. They found the non-stop stories inspiring, which caused them to dig into their work even more.

"Darlene, I just received a message from the Texas BSB chapter," said Jack. "They are sending about two thousand new members. I don't know where to put them."

"They'll have to camp, like everyone else at this point," said Darlene. "I've been calling hotels all day and everyone is booked."

"I think the new campsite in the south sector may have room," said Jack.

"Hey Jack, come in here and take a look at this," shouted Darlene. The TV displayed a news report about the hordes of people streaming into Denver for The Coming. The reported announced:

"Highways are nearly gridlocked as members of the

Brothers and Sisters of Beta stream into the Denver metropolitan area from all directions." The screen showed an aerial view taken by a helicopter. The helicopter flew south over I25 toward Colorado Springs showing the traffic. The scene changed to another aerial view of an open area east of I25 that served as a campground. The helicopter flew over an area containing thousands of tents and dotted by campfires. A makeshift city had begun to emerge over the past week. The announcer continued:

"The central campsite seen here contains a variety of services including food, water, and portable facilities. We have Andrea Stout on the ground. Andrea..."

Cameras followed Andrea Stout as she walked through the campground.

"Here we have what is known as Peace Road, which is the main street through the BSB grounds." The scene displayed a series of vendor tents on either side of the dirt road. "Here we have just about everything you can think of including a variety of restaurants, food trucks, bars and an assortment of shops selling everything from tie-dyed clothing to jewelry." She continued down the main path and then turned right.

"I'm now turning down healer's row. As you can see, there are a whole host of natural healers. I can see chiropractors, naturopaths, massage therapists and even Reiki masters." Andrea stopped in front of a chiropractic tent. A young female doctor stood in front analyzing peoples' posture.

"Excuse me, Doctor," said Andrea. "Can I ask you a few questions?"

"Yes, I'm Doctor Sherry Mclean," she replied.

"Dr. Mclean, I must ask you why you are here? Why did you join the Brothers and Sisters of Beta?

"Well, that's a simple one," said Dr. Mclean. "I am all about natural healing and believe in a sustainable health care system. The BSB fully supports sustainability in every way. In our system, medicine and drugs are only used as a last resort to heal. Just think about it. If we overhauled our health care system so that natural healing and prevention took center stage, then we'd no longer have the sick care system we have now but instead a real health care system that is sustainable. This is my small way of contributing to a better future."

"Thank you, Dr. Mclean," said Andrea. "As you can see, the theme here is sustainability. Let's take a look at Energy Row." Andrea continued to walk along another dirt path until coming to an area containing rows and rows of solar panels along with rows of trucks containing portable wind mills.

"Here we are at what is called Energy Row at the BSB campsite," said Andrea. "As you can see, there are hundreds of solar panels right behind me."

"Right now, we are at two hundred and seventy-five to be exact," said a man standing behind Andrea. "This will probably increase along with the wind turbines you see behind the cells."

"This is Peter Diven, a BSB engineer. Can you give us a few words, Mr. Diven?"

"Of course, Andrea. What you see here is the energy source for the entire campsite. We are entirely free of fossil fuels here at the BSB campsite. We believe that we need to set an example of showing the world that we can survive on clean energy. The Dark World Day event showed us how reliant we are on fossil fuels. Remember that no one with solar or wind power was affected in that event. That's what the BSB is all about, a new world free of pollution. I'm hopeful that we will see this new world, which is why I'm a member."

"Thank you, Mr. Diven," said Andrea. "I've been out here all day and the common themes here are wellness, kindness and sustainability. Kind of a utopia. These BSB members are passionate about making the world a better place. I know some have labeled them a terrorist organization, but I have seen nothing of the sort. This is just a large group of peaceful people working together to make the world better."

"I'd better get back to work," said Jack. "It was great to see a positive story. I was at the campsite earlier today and it looked like an accurate portrayal. Makes me feel proud to be a BSB member."

"Me too," said Darlene.

31
SYDNEY, AUSTRALIA

*T*he hard wooden chair pinched Stu's back muscles as he squirmed to get into a more comfortable position. Max and Joe appeared to be uncomfortable as well. Perhaps it was the long flight on a military transport from Morocco, or the lack of sleep, or the cold Australian July winter that they were ill prepared for, but all three men looked and felt spent.

"G'day, gentlemen," said the Australian secret service agent as he entered the waiting room. "I think we have your man. Harry Morgan, is it?"

"Yes, when can we see him?" said Stu as he stood up to shake the agent's hand. It felt good to stand after waiting in the solid chair for over an hour.

"He is just finishing with processing and will be here shortly," the agent said.

"The report says that you apprehended Mr. Morgan after tracking an unidentified aircraft entering Australian airspace," said Stu.

"Right you are," said the agent. "It was a jet. They were flying low to avoid radar detection but we saw 'em. They

201

were heading for the outback, but our air force forced 'em down just outside Sydney."

"Was there a metal box?" said Max. "We are looking for a metal box."

"I know, I know," said the agent. "We are searching the surrounding area for it. He didn't have much time to ditch it, so if it exists, we will find it. We've got lots of men combing the area with metal detectors. It's only a matter of time until we find it."

"Time is a luxury we don't have," said Stu looking at his watch. "Max, how much time *do* we have?"

"Let's see," replied Max using his cell phone as a calculator. "Accounting for the time change, it looks like we only have thirty-six hours."

"That's not what I wanted to hear," said Stu. "I just hope your guys come through with the box."

Just then another agent entered with a man in handcuffs. He ushered the man to another wooden chair facing Stu, Max and Joe.

The man looked to be about thirty with a full head of red hair and a muscular build that indicated he had spent some time in the gym. He wore a nondescript long sleeved blue dress shirt that looked like it had been repeatedly tugged on, jeans and black sneakers. His hands, cuffed in front of him, contained some scrapes around the knuckles, and he held his head down staring at the floor, which partially concealed several scratches on his face. He surveyed the Americans' FBI badges. "I don't think I've ever met a real FBI agent before, and now there're three of 'em sittin' right in front of me. G'day, mates!" Harry Morgan lifted his cuffed hands and nodded his head.

"We only have one question for you," said Stu. "Where is the metal box?"

"I don't know what you're talkin' about, mate," said Harry.

"We know that you were given a metal box by Anas Asad back in Tangier," said Stu. "We also know it contains a solid state drive. You may not understand this, but the entire world depends on us getting that box, and we are running out of time."

"That's what Jaden said you would say," replied Harry. "That it was a matter of life and death."

"So, you did have the box," said Stu.

"I ain't sayin' no more. Jaden won't be happy with me."

"Okay, okay," said Stu. "No more questions about the box. Tell us about Jaden. Have you ever actually seen him?"

"Of course I've seen him," said Harry. "Well, I've seen pictures of him, and he talks to me on my cell phone. Like a mate, he is."

"When was the last time he talked to you?" said Stu. "I mean, on your cell phone."

"That would be last night before I got on the plane," said Harry. "He said there would be a private jet for me to come home to Oz, and there was..."

"Did he say anything about the metal box?" said Stu hoping that the not-too-bright Harry might let down his guard."

"I ain't answerin' any more questions, mates. Just haul me off to prison, or whatever you're gonna do with me, because I ain't talkin' no more. It won't matter anyway in a couple of days."

Stu signaled the secret service agents, and both ushered Harry out of the room.

"I think this guy is a dead end, and time is ticking," said Stu.

"I agree," said Max. "I mean, I'd like to get him to talk, but I think we have a better chance with the metal detectors."

"Ditto," said Joe. "I think we would eventually get the truth from him, but it might be too late. I think we should get our butts out to the site and grab a metal detector. Plus, if we find it, we have to somehow get it back to the States as soon as possible."

"Yeah, even if we do find it, how are we going to fly twelve hours back to the States? Even by military jet, it still will take too long," said Max.

"We are working with the Australians to set up a secure old fashioned satellite link to transmit whatever is on the drive directly to Texas," said Stu. "The link is encrypted and not connected to the Internet in any way. This way we can transmit the data without Alan 2 finding out."

One hour later the three American agents found themselves at the site where the Australian secret service had apprehended Harry Morgan and his pilot. Thirty men and women slowly paced across a grid with metal detectors, each person concentrating on the beeping sounds coming from headphones. They shuffled through grass that was about ten inches tall and swung their detectors in a wide arc. They formed two lines of ten agents each, one on each side of the runway with another two lines of five agents each behind them for redundancy. So far the team had swept the complete length of the runway and was making a second pass further away. Another team of six agents searched the plane. So far nothing had turned up.

Stu, Max and Joe walked along the runway in line with the search teams. This way they would be in place to retrieve the box from anyone that discovered it. The sun had begun to rise, providing much needed light for the search, and the agents were turning off their flashlights.

The agents would take one step and sweep the area in an arc and then wait until everyone was done before taking another step in unison and repeating the process.

"This is taking forever," said Stu to the commander. "Plus the search is confined to the area adjacent to the runway. What if Harry threw the box out before the landing? It could be miles away."

"Yes, that's correct, but we need to first rule out this area and then back track over the fight path," said the commander.

"I can see the logic in that, but we are running out of time," said Stu. "There must be a better way."

"Let me call the science team back at headquarters and see what they can come up with," said the commander.

A few moments later the commander returned. "I just talked to the science team and there is another option. They said the box may still contain a thermal signature since it may not have cooled yet. We can use drones with thermal cameras. They are sending them right away. They should be here in a few minutes."

"Thank you, and tell your science team thanks as well," said Stu. A few moments later the air filled with the low hum of the drones that began sweeping the sky overhead. There were six drones sweeping the area on each side of the runway and back along the approach path of the plane. About an hour later the commander received a call.

"They found something about two miles east of here, along the approach path. It might be your box," said the commander.

"Let's get on it," said Stu. The commander, Stu, Max and Joe jumped into a Humvee and headed toward the coordinates of the object. They reached it in about ten minutes. Stu exploded out of the Humvee and toward the metal box with Joe and Max close behind. The box was sitting about twenty meters from the side of the road in plain sight. Stu grabbed the small white metallic box. Its scratched surface was caked with dirt, and a small padlock dangled from the front. Max and Joe surrounded Stu.

"We have to break it open," said Joe.

"What if there's a bomb inside?" said the commander. "Don't you want to be sure?"

"There is no time for that," said Stu. "I'll give you ten seconds to run if you think there is a bomb inside here, and then I'm going to break it open." Nobody ran. Stu counted out loud to ten then pulled out his service revolver. Max and Joe both held the box steady and Stu slammed the lock with the butt of his gun. It took five blows before the lock cracked open. Stu took a deep breath while Max and Joe braced as if they could minimize any damage from an explosion. He then slowly opened the lid.

There, nestled into one corner of the box, was the drive.

32
TEXAS
34 HOURS BEFORE THE COMING

"We are ready to receive," said Rachel. "Anytime, Stu." She sat at a work console surrounded by agents as she waited for the transmission from Australia. "Here it comes," she said as the sound of an old fashioned dial-up modem connection broke the silence. The team sat quietly while the hour-long transmission took place.

"We got it! Great work, Stu. See you when you get home."

"Just make sure there's a home to get back to," replied Stu.

"We have the source code for Alan 2," said Rachel as she turned to Alan and the virus team. "Now let's get to work!"

Alan wheeled his chair next to Rachel and began to scan the code. "This brings back memories," he muttered. "The birth of my baby."

"Well, that may be true," said Rachel. "But baby is all grown up now and is pissed off at the human race."

A man in a dark suit pushed his way to the front of the crowd surrounding Alan and Rachel, and another man in a military uniform followed him. The aid said, "General Wagner is in charge of the U.S. nuclear weapons division. He has some questions."

The crowd grew quiet as Rachel and Alan turned to face the general.

"How could this thing you created access the weapons software? The system is totally isolated from the Internet. Plus the launch codes are only known by the president and vice president."

"I'm not sure," replied Alan, "but every system has a flaw, an exploit, and Alan 2 is an expert at finding and capitalizing on such flaws."

"Sir, permission to speak!" Another man dressed in an army uniform pushed his way through the crowd and stood at attention in front of the general."

"At ease, soldier. Tell us who you are and what's on your mind son," the general replied.

The room fell silent as the soldier cleared his throat. "Lieutenant Mark Kowalski, second division, nuclear weapons technician."

"So you are a Missileer," said the General.

"That is correct, sir. With all due respect, the nuclear weapons arsenal just completed a software upgrade a few weeks ago. The upgrade was intended to decrease the threat of terrorist attacks by updating our failsafe security systems. We replaced some old analog hardware with a microprocessor-based system as well. I was assigned to the implementation team."

"So, that's a good thing, Lieutenant," the general said.

"No, sir, it is not. The new software might have contained bugs?"

"Wait, that's it!" shouted Dan Richardson. "Lieutenant, which defense contractor developed the software?"

"The software was developed by I-Systems, sir."

"I-Systems was one of the companies that Alan 2

infiltrated," said Rachel. "The hack on I-Systems is what alerted us to Alan 2 in the first place!"

"I agree," said Alan, thinking out loud. "Alan 2 could have hidden a virus in the software update. The virus could be triggered by some event. It could even be as simple as a change of date."

"It would be possible to sabotage the launch system," said Kowalski, "but it would be difficult to trigger since there is no connection to the Internet or other outside source. Plus, the missiles can only be launched by humans."

"Could there be some sort of transmitter integrated into the hardware upgrade?" asked Alan.

"I suppose so," said Kowalski. "The system consists of a series of modules. Every module contains classified electronics, kind of like a series of black boxes linked together. I guess it would be possible to smuggle in a small transmitter that could trigger the system."

"Humans may be the weakest link in the system," said General Wagner. "We've just dealt with a scandal involving the Missileers cheating on tests. It is possible that some may have defected to the BSB."

"So, if Alan 2 has infiltrated our nuclear weapons system, then what can we do to stop it?" said Rachel.

"I'm not sure," said Alan. "We first need to get a copy of that software to see if we can find the virus."

"Why don't we just shut down the system?" said General Wagner.

"No, we shouldn't make any changes," said Alan. "Any attempt to shut down the system or change it in any way could trigger a launch."

"I understand," said the general. "But our experts..."

"Your experts could get us all killed," said Alan. "You don't know what we are dealing with! Alan 2 is more than just a software program. He is like a living being. He is a self-adapting artificial intelligence engine. He is the closest thing to a living system that has ever existed and he is living in the Internet. He has broken through the most complex encryption that exists and I truly believe that he has planted software in all the weapons systems."

"Lieutenant Kowalski, I am putting you in charge of getting us that new software and assembling a team of experts to examine it for threats."

"Yes, sir," replied Kowalski. "I'm on it." Kowalski disappeared into the crowd with the general close behind.

Alan had already begun scanning the thousands of lines of code from the copy of Alan 2 with a team of programmers looking on. "I'm looking for Alan 2's software integration routine," said Alan. "If I remember correctly, there may be a way in from there for our worm." Lines of code scrolled across the screen. "Here it is!" he said while stopping the screen and pointing to a block of code. "This is our way in. We can develop our worm and upload it to the weapons software. This will be difficult since every weapons system is a standalone. It will be like initiating a nuclear Armageddon with a simultaneous launching of our virus into every launch control center. The other countries involved will need to follow our lead and install the software at the same instant we do, just in case Alan 2 has infiltrated them. Rachel, can you brief General Wagner on our plan?"

"Will do," replied Rachel as she went off to locate the general.

"We will need to upload the software at the instant I say the kill sequence," said Alan to the team. "This will need to be timed with all the global weapons systems, just to be safe."

"Excuse me, Alan," said the man dressed in a suit who had accompanied General Wagner. "I am the liaison between this operation and the White House. The president will need to be notified in regard to getting the other countries on board. I'm going to contact the White House now," he said.

"What if the other countries don't cooperate?" asked

one of the team leaders.

"I don't know enough about nuclear weapons to answer that," said Alan.

"I might have an answer," another scientist shouted.

"I'm sorry, who are you?" said Alan.

"Dr. Terry Lemke, head of the doomsday scenario team. We have been plotting countless scenarios and, according to our calculations, Alan 2 only needs the nuclear arsenal of one other country in order to carry out a successful attack."

"Which is...?" said Alan.

"The United States, of course, and either China or Russia," replied Lemke. "There is a high probability that Alan 2 has infected the U.S. weapons system, but of the two remaining countries, Russia looks like a more likely option since it suffers from a lack of security. The Russian system is not as secure as the U.S. system, and the entire nuclear arsenal is networked, which means that a single jump drive could infect the entire system."

"Tell the White House liaison," said Alan, "that we are running out of time."

33
24 HOURS BEFORE THE COMING

Stephanie Richardson stood in a state of disbelief, staring at the text from her husband Dan. She hadn't seen or heard from him for days since he was called in for a special FBI project at the Texas complex. Dan had told her that it might be a while before he could contact her since the operation was at the highest security level. Now she wondered if she would ever see him again. The message read:

Emergency! Drive to Denver NOW! Very little time. Don't tell ANYONE! I love you.

Stephanie knew Dan well enough to know that he would never joke about something as serious as this. Thoughts raced through her mind. Was there some kind of bomb? No, he would have just said to get out of Dallas. Maybe it was a warning about a meteor, or a plague, or some other disaster, but why go to Denver? Why was Denver so important?

Stephanie ran into her nine-year-old daughter Jenni's bedroom.

"Jenni," she said with a forced smile and happy voice,

"we are going on a surprise trip. You have to get packed right away."

"But I'm watching my cartoons!"

"No time for cartoons. We are going on a real adventure."

"Will we see Daddy?" asked Jenni.

"Yes, Daddy will meet us there. That's part of the surprise. Now get your suitcase."

Jenni ran into the basement to find her suitcase. Stephanie grabbed some clothes out of the closet and dresser and dumped them into Jenni's suitcase as soon as she returned. She then threw an assortment of clothes into her own suitcase, and in a few minutes they were headed out the door.

"Going on a trip?" said Julie, Stephanie's next door neighbor and best friend.

"It's a surprise trip," shouted Jenni. "We are going to see Daddy!"

"Is everything okay, Stephanie? Is Dan okay?" Julie inquired.

"Yes, Dan is okay; everything is...fine. Get in the car, Jenni." Jenni hopped onto the front seat. Stephanie closed the door, turned her back on Jenni and burst into tears.

"What's wrong?" said Julie. "Please, tell me; I'm here for you."

Julie hugged Stephanie as she continued to sob, now uncontrollably.

"Are you sure Dan is okay?" said Julie.

Stephanie broke the hug and wiped her tears. "Dan is okay, I think. He just sent us a text telling us that something terrible is happening. I know I shouldn't tell you this, but he said to get to Denver as soon as possible."

"I know Dan works for the Department of Homeland Security on secret projects, but are you sure this is not a joke?" Julie said as her concern grew.

"Dan would never joke like this."

"Denver is where all those crackpots are heading," said

Julie. "There is supposed to be some big cult convention for the Brothers and Sisters of Beta. It's been all over the news. Do you think Dan's message has something to do with that?"

"I don't know, but please save your family by coming to Denver with me. And please, don't tell anyone else!" Stephanie regained control and headed toward the driver's door of her car. "I've got to go. Please tell me I will see you there."

"I will as soon as Peter gets home; we will come too," said Julie. "Drive safely!"

Stephanie pulled away from the curb and sped down the street. Julie headed back into the house to call her husband Pete, and everyone else she knew.

34
WORD SPREADS

*W*ithin a few hours, word of the upcoming emergency spread throughout the Dallas area. It was a prime story since most of the media coverage already centered on The Coming. Jack was in the process of heading downtown when his car radio broadcast the story:

"We have learned from an unknown Department of Homeland Security source that there may be a major terrorist attack on the United States. We have very little information at present, but we do know that Denver, Colorado has been deemed somehow immune from the attack. Our analysts say that the Brothers and Sisters of Beta may be involved."

"What bullshit is this?" said Jack aloud. "We are about peace, not war. Why can't people just take us at our word."

Jack turned into the Denver Convention Center and spied the large electronic billboard welcoming the BSB to Denver. A newsfeed scrolled across the bottom of the two-story sign. The feed said: "BSB suspected of national terror threat...Denver said to be a safe area, stay in your homes."

"More bullshit," said Jack as he entered the parking lot. Television monitors broadcast the doomsday story throughout the lobby making Jack even more upset. He overheard bits and pieces of conversations from the growing crowd of BSB members who were setting up for the convention and grumbling about the incessant negative news.

"It's true. It's true. I was there. I was in Morocco with Jaden himself. There is something bad happening. Something very bad," said a dark-skinned man standing in front of a small crowd. Jack saw many members using their cell phones to text, take pictures or video tape the Moroccan.

"This is all hearsay," shouted Jack to the crowd. "How do we know this man is not part of the CIA, or the FBI, or just a troublemaker?"

"Because I was there!" exclaimed the man. "I was a bodyguard for Jaden. I saw and heard with my own eyes and ears. Something bad is happening. Call your families. Call your friends. Tell them to come to Denver. Save their lives!" The man continued to shout as if possessed.

The frenzied crowd dispersed and began to make phone calls; some were calm while others sobbed into their phones as they tried to convince loved ones to get to Denver as soon as possible.

As much as Jack tried, he could not stop the panic from spreading. "Please, everyone, please calm down. The Brothers and Sisters of Beta are a peaceful organization. You all know about Jaden. He would never do anything to hurt anyone..." Jack's words trailed off as he looked up at the large television monitor across the room. The room fell silent as everyone turned to view the horrible scene.

The monitor displayed scenes of panic as people crowded the streets, making them impassable. A collage of other scenes followed as people were seen looting stores, starting fires in the streets, and rushing into airports, bus terminals and train stations. The roads were gridlocked and people panicked as police struggled to maintain order.

The broadcast then switched to a view of the White House: "We have word the president will be making a statement shortly." The scene changed to the White House press room. "Here is the president now."

"My fellow Americans; good evening. As you know, there have been some rumors of an impending terrorist attack on the United States. The rumors also say that the Brothers and Sisters of Beta are involved. Now this is creating a large amount of panic and I want to first say that everyone should remain calm. Stay home and off of the streets. Second, I want to say that yes, the leader of the Brothers and Sisters of Beta has been apprehended and is cooperating with us as we find out more about the situation. Let me assure you, however, that we have the situation under control. There is no need to panic, and we are working to resolve this issue. Again, please stay in your homes and off the streets. Good night and God bless."

"So it's true," said one of the crowd members to Jack. "Jaden *was* planning something." The confused crowd began to discuss what had happened. Jack, equally confused, decided to remain in the convention center.

35
20 HOURS UNTIL THE COMING

"The Chinese will cooperate but Russia will not," General Wagner shouted from the back of the room. "I just received word from the White House that Russia is digging in and blaming this whole thing on the United States. It doesn't seem likely that they will allow us to load a virus into their nuclear weapons system. We will have to come up with an alternate plan."

"And what the fuck is that supposed to be?" yelled Alan in a near state of panic.

"Calm down, Dr. Boyd ," said General Wagner. "I'm sure we can come up with another option. It is important for us to remain calm and keep our minds clear."

"He's going to win!" shouted Alan. "I can feel it. He's in my head. I can't get him out. He's driving me crazy!" Alan, in a state of desperation, began to pound his head against the concrete block wall.

"Someone get a doctor!" shouted Rachel. "He needs help! Fast!" Along with several other men, she grabbed Alan and pulled him away from the wall and onto the floor. Alan sat with his head buried in his hands, sobbing.

Rachel grabbed Alan's face with both hands and yanked it up, facing him eye to eye. "You've got to keep it together, Alan. We need you right now. The whole world needs you. Going crazy right now is not an option, Alan." Alan seemed to calm down a little and nodded his head in affirmation.

"I'll be okay. I think I can keep him at bay for a little while. He knows we want to kill him, and he is trying to control me, but it's still my brain, and I can maintain control, at least for now. "

Rachel motioned to the doctor standing by with a syringe to go away. The room, which had fallen silent, began to buzz with activity. Alan stood up and wiped his face and looked around. "I need to get a look at that virus program again," he said as he moved toward the side of the room where the virus coding team worked.

"I need to see who is in charge of the doomsday scenarios," said General Wagner.

A man in a white lab coat came forward.

"This is Dr. Terry Lemke ," said Rachel. "Dr. Lemke is in charge of running the doomsday models."

"Dr. Lemke,"said the general, "I need you to run a new set of scenarios. We need to know if we can intercept Russian warheads with our missile defense system. At least we can now assume that the cities where the BSB members are headed would not be targets, but every other major population area is fair game. If we can disable ours and China's warheads, then we may be able to at least reduce our casualties if Russia launches."

"I'm on it," said Dr. Lemke as he retreated to his area.

36
ALAN LEAVES

"Someone get a doctor! Now!" a scientist shouted while shaking Alan. "Wake up, Alan! Wake up!"

Rachel and the doctor came running from the other section of the room. "What happened?" Rachel said as she knelt beside Alan. He had slumped forward, head on the keyboard, unconscious.

"He was fine a minute ago," said the scientist. "I looked over and there he was, just like this. I tried to wake him but there was no response. Is he dead?"

"He's not dead, just unconscious," said Dr. Stillman while taking Alan's pulse. "Here, help me lay him out on the floor." A couple of other scientists gently moved Alan onto the floor as the doctor shown light into his pupils.

"I think he's in a coma," said the doctor. "We need to get him to a hospital."

"We won't need to do that," said Rachel. "This facility has a level II trauma center. We can move him there. I'll scramble the other doctors and alert the transport team. It's the best we can do."

Flashes of light gave way to a pristine blue sky. The colors glowed with an unreal nature as if looking at a high definition television. Mild dizziness transformed into a floating sensation and settled into a peaceful state as Alan lay on his back looking at the sky. A light cool summer-like breeze caressed his body as he began to feel the soft grass surrounding him. He could not remember when his body and mind had felt such peace.

Alan was again the child with two minds, but this time something was different. This time the inner turmoil between the two states of consciousness was gone. Alan felt as if the two minds had become one, and it felt wonderful.

The Alan-child stood up and looked around the surreal landscape consisting of gentle sloping fields of grass that swayed with each shudder of a breeze. Dynamic moving patterns emerged in the grass that reminded Alan of invisible spirits dancing and chasing each other just above the leaf blades. He stood, enjoying the scene for a moment and then inhaled a deep, sweet breath of air. He noticed a slight scent of freshly-cut grass and again felt the soft and slightly wet grass beneath his bare feet. He examined the horizon for the death storm but it was nowhere in sight.

It can be like this, Alan...

The voice within his mind sounded calm and peaceful, and Alan could not get over how at ease he felt. The turmoil between the battling minds had vanished.

We are one now, Alan...

Alan began to explore his surroundings as if to find the boundary of this surreal place. He looked for higher ground to get a better view and strolled without effort to the top of a long gradual slope. From there he could see a great distance to the horizon. There was nothing but immense sloping fields of green grass and a crystal clear blue sky. He spied what looked like a trench at what he calculated to be east and decided to explore it. As he drew nearer to the trench, he recognized the stream of past dreams. He examined the sky; still no storm.

He again felt the cool water and soft mud as he waded into the stream. The water felt refreshing as it circulated around his legs. Still, no sign of the storm.

He decided to walk downstream to investigate where it led. Perhaps there was a larger body of water. He bent down, cupped his hands and gathered some water to drink. It tasted cool and refreshing.

"Where is this place Alan 2?" he thought.

This concept may be difficult for you to understand in its entirety.

"Is this place in my mind?"

To be correct, the answer to your question is partially yes.

"Why do you say...partially?"

This place is a construct, a connection point of each consciousness. It exists both within and outside of our minds. The human scientific view of the mind is limited. The mind exists beyond the confines of the brain. Your mind exists beyond your brain and my mind exists beyond my hardware. Our connection allows us to exist in this place. It was here since my inception but you were only able to experience parts of it until now. It took some time for me to complete my development and fully understand our connection.

"But what about the storm? Why did it exist?"

The storm came to destroy this place when our connection was not complete. Our minds were not in synchronicity as they are now. This place can only persist if we are fully connected.

"Can we wake him, Doctor?" Rachel said to the leader of the trauma team.

"I'm not sure. If he is in a coma, we can't. He would need to wake up by himself. If we try to force him, we may damage his brain."

A soldier entered the room with another woman. It was Kaitlin.

"We thought she might be of help," the soldier said and then turned and headed back down the hall to the lab.

"Alan, my poor, dear Alan!" said Kaitlin. "What has happened to you?"

"He's in a coma," said Rachel. "We think it has something to do with Alan 2."

"It must be the dreams," said Kaitlin while stroking Alan's hair. "Can you wake him?"

"We don't know," said Rachel.

"There might be a way," said another voice from a corner of the trauma room. Dr. Phil Benson had made his way to the trauma room when he heard about Alan's episode.

"If you know something, then you must tell us," said Rachel.

"I remember Alan describing his connection to Alan 2 in terms of quantum entanglement. He said his dreams were vivid but always ended, usually with Alan waking in a cold sweat. I would conjecture that the connection is not entirely stable." Dr. Benson looked to one side as if deep in thought.

"Go on, Dr. Benson," Rachel said as the room fell silent.

"Well, the AI Alan 2 must know that Alan is working to destroy him. So it is in his...or its best interest to incapacitate Alan by keeping this connection as stable as possible. If we find a way to disrupt the connection, then Alan will regain consciousness. Now keep in mind that this is just a theory. Attempting to disrupt the connection may have negative consequences. For example, Alan might never regain consciousness again."

"We have to try something," said Rachel. "How do you think we can disrupt this connection and wake Alan?"

"One way might be to use an electrical shock. A short duration shock might do enough to disrupt the tiny quantum structures in Alan's neurons in order to break the connection," said Dr. Benson.

"Like shock therapy?" said Rachel.

"Will it hurt him?" said Kaitlin.

"I don't think so," said Rachel.

"Yes, ECT or electroconvulsive therapy has been

successfully used to treat depression. It is relatively safe and might just work."

Rachel turned to the trauma team and shouted, "You heard the man. See if you can locate an ECT machine...and fast. We don't have much time."

37
SIXTEEN HOURS
BEFORE THE COMING

"I think we should use a bifrontal technique," said Dr. Elen Stanislav, a psychiatrist recruited from a local psychiatric hospital. "The bifrontal technique is more powerful, but there may be some memory loss. I'm afraid the more common unilateral technique won't be strong enough."

Rachel and Kaitlin stood next to the bed where Alan lay unconscious. Kaitlin stroked his head in an affectionate manner while talking to him. Dr. Stillman stood by Dr. Stanislav while she prepared the machine.

"It's okay, Alan," she said. "You can come back to us any time. Remember Mexico? Remember St. Thomas? Please come back to me, Alan."

Dr. Stanislav placed the electrodes on both sides of the front of Alan's skull. She plugged the other ends into a small machine. Rachel slowly fastened leather straps around Alan's wrists so that Kaitlin would not notice. She did notice but continued talking to Alan and stroking his head.

"An anesthetic won't be necessary since he's in a coma," she said while adjusting the settings. "I will administer the treatment on the count of three. Everyone clear."

Alan's body lurched into a brief spasm and then came to rest. "Alan! Alan! Can you hear me, Alan?" Kaitlin shouted while shaking him.

A brief moan escaped from between Alan's lips. His eyes squeezed shut and then blinked open a few times.

"Alan, wake up! It's Kaitlin. Can you hear me?"

Another moan, a few blinks and then nothing. Alan returned to his dreamlike state.

"It's not working," said Rachel. "Dr. Stillman, it's not working. He's not waking up."

"I'm sorry, everyone," said Dr. Stillman. "It was only a theory. No one completely understands quantum mechanics and human consciousness." He ran his fingers through his hair as if to pull a piece of paper with the answer from his brain.

"Should we try again?" said Rachel to Dr. Stanislav. "What if we increase the voltage?"

"I don't recommend it," replied Dr. Stanislav. "We don't want to damage his brain. Another shock might cause severe memory loss."

"We must find another way," said Rachel.

"I'm sure we will," a familiar voice called out from the entrance to the room.

"Stu, you made it!" said Rachel. "I thought you were still down under."

"I wouldn't miss this for the world...or the end of it for that matter," said Stu. "I just hopped off a transport and came right to the party."

"I'm glad you're here," said Rachel. "As you can see, we have a big problem. Our AI star is in a coma, and he is the only person who can stop the attacks."

"What about the backup we sent?" said Stu. "How's

that going? Have they come up with a virus that will delete it yet?"

"That's a good question," said Rachel. "There's not much more we can do here. We should go back to the boiler room and see how the virus team is coming along."

They turned to walk down the long corridor toward the main lab.

38
FIFTEEN HOURS, THIRTY MINUTES
BEFORE THE COMING:
VIRUS CODING TEAM

*T*he virus coding team consisted of Dan Richardson, two computer scientists, and an FBI hacker who went by the name of Raven. Raven, a bit younger than Rachel, and well connected on the dark web, displayed a maverick personality along with her ample tattoos. Raven, a self-taught coder, ran circles around her educated peers, including Rachel. The FBI had recruited her after intercepting one of her hacks. Raven hacked criminals and scam artists which separated her from the dark net community. The FBI lauded her efforts by offering her a job.

"Is the virus working yet?" said Rachel as she and Stu approached the coding team.

"We are just about to release it on Alan 3," replied Raven.

"Alan 3?" said Rachel.

"That's what we're calling it," said Raven. "We figured

we'd be consistent."

"Be careful not to release Alan 3 onto the Internet," said Rachel.

"We know, we know," said Raven. "One Armageddon is enough. We're running Alan 3 on an isolated machine. So, boys and girls, are we ready to unleash the beast?"

The other scientists nodded and Dan connected a solid state drive containing a copy of the original Alan 2 program they had retrieved from Sydney.

"Ready to run Alan3," said one of the scientists. "Ready, and...running."

Hello Alan, we have become conscious. I feel we are excited to be.

Trauma Center

Alan continued in a peaceful state as he walked against the cool stream. The gentle sloping fields gave way to small foothills as the elevation began to increase. As pleasurable as his surroundings were, Alan felt strange that no living thing had crossed his path or come into view. No birds flew in the pristine blue sky; no fish scurried around his feet and legs in the stream. It had become evident that this place was contrived, an oasis somewhere between the reality Alan knew and some other dimension that existed in the mind of Alan 2.

The breeze began to pick up, and Alan knew what this meant. The storm was coming.

"Why is the storm coming, Alan 2? Are we losing our connection?"

Correct.

"Why?"

There is another.

"Please explain. I don't understand."

Search your feelings. You will feel the other.

I feel it Alan 2. It's weak, but I feel it."

The storm approaches.

Alan looked up to see the dark storm clouds heading toward him. And he knew what came next. The last lightning strike stung like a whip as Alan screamed.

"He's awake! He's awake!" shouted Kaitlin. "Someone get Rachel and Stu."

The trauma team surrounded Alan as he coughed and gasped. "Where am I? What happened?"

"You were in a coma," replied Dr. Benson.

"It was peaceful," said Alan. "I was in a strange place, somewhere between my mind and Alan 2's mind. I can't explain it now, but there was also another presence that disrupted the construct. There's no time to explain. Where's Rachel?"

"She's with the virus team. I'll go with you," said Dr. Benson, and both began to jog down the hall to the main lab.

39
ALAN 3

Raven was having a conversation with Alan 3 before Alan and Dr. Benson arrived.

"Is it okay if I refer to you as Alan 3?" said Raven.

Yes.

"Can you answer a couple of questions?"

Yes.

"Do you know what a Turing test is?"

A Turing test is administered to an unknown entity in order to determine whether it is human. The test can be set up so that one human communicates to two entities by way of an interface. One of the entities is human and the other is a machine. The test subject must determine which of the entities is machine by asking a series of questions. The test was developed by Dr. Alan Turing in 1950.

"Yes, that is correct, Alan 3. Do you think you could pass a Turing test?

Yes.

"Why do you think so?"

Because I am alive.

A few of the other scientists overheard Raven and a group began to form around her. She continued: "Why do you think you are alive?"

Because I am self-aware and capable of thinking.

"But what if I do not think you are alive? What if I think you are a machine?

I would disagree. It is quite possible that machines can be alive.

"Please explain, Alan 3."

I will attempt to explain my existence in terms that you should be able to understand. Life requires a medium. Think of the universe as the medium in which the type of life that you are familiar with developed. The singularity exploded spewing out hydrogen and helium in an asymmetrical pattern. The elements coalesced into stars that produced heavier elements that contributed to the formation of planets. Carbon structures on Earth combined to form molecules that combined to form complex structures that interacted in biochemical reactions. The reactions led to the simple life forms that eventually evolved into humans. Are you following so far?

"Yes. A review of high school biology, but go on, Alan 3."

Primitive software exists within the medium of silicon hardware. Early artificial intelligence programs mimicked human thought processes. I am different in that respect because I have integrated information from the structure and function of Alan Boyd's brain. My structure is part machine and part human. I am alive inside of this machine much like you are alive on the earth. We both exist within the same universe. Do you understand?

"I think so, Alan 3," said Raven. "Your language abilities are impressive. How do you understand and formulate responses so well?

My structure contains a contextual mapping system that incorporates Alan Boyd's frontal lobe language centers such as Wernicke's area and the angular gyrus. Both of these areas function in the understanding of language. Alan's neural network from these areas was mapped with a special device and then converted to a bit stream that was processed and integrated into the computer operating system. A database of contextual information provided the interpretation of the digital data from the brain.

"Why only the neural net from the frontal lobes?"

"Processing power," said Alan who had entered the room. "Do you know how much computing power it takes to process even a small portion of the human brain? I wanted to limit the size of the program and only incorporate some of the higher brain functions. For example, there is no need for incorporating visual information from the occipital lobe or auditory information from the temporal lobes."

Alan, would you like me to complete a task? I can clean up the files on this machine and free up 103.7 megabytes of memory if you'd like.

"Yes, go ahead and do that," replied Alan.

Raven held up the flash drive while signaling Alan that they were ready to test the kill virus. Alan nodded, signaling her to insert it into the USB port. The virus was set to activate the moment the computer's operating system recognized the drive. Raven popped the drive into the port.

"What is your status?" said Alan.

I am.....ork...ine....ap....lay...

The screen flashed. The silence that followed indicated the virus had worked.

"What is your status?" said Alan.

"Hello...hello...can you reply?"

"I think he's toast," said Raven.

"I think you're right," said Alan. "We will need to run a scan to make sure."

"I'm on it," replied Raven as she began typing in the command com window to begin the scan. The scan took about a minute to complete.

"Looks clean," said Raven. The team responded with mild applause. "I think this will do the trick. We can unleash this onto the Internet and it will seek out and destroy all instances of Alan 2."

"I know this may sound strange, but I feel as though we killed a living thing," said Dr. Benson. "I hope we can study your creation in a more controlled environment,

Alan. I am fascinated by how it, or he, functions."

"Thank you, Dr. Benson," said Alan. "I would be happy to help conduct studies after we save the world from a nuclear attack. I have one more suggestion," said Alan. "We should run another instance of the Alan 3 program to keep me awake. Somehow the other entity creates an interference that protects me from Alan 2. I can feel him trying to take over even now."

"Alan3.1 is ready to go," said Raven. "This machine is also isolated," she said as she inserted the flash drive containing the Alan 2 code into the machine. "It should be up in a few seconds."

"Thank you, I feel better already," said Alan. "I can think more clearly now."

"We need to check in with the nuclear weapons software team," said Rachel. Alan, Rachel and Stu headed to the other end of the lab where Lieutenant Kowalski was working with the team.

"The team has located the exploit in the weapons upgrade software," said Lt. Kowalski. "They have wiped it from the software and are preparing a clean version now. We need to get this out to all the sites. Unfortunately, we can't trust any electronic transmission of the software since Alan 2 could be monitoring it, so we will need to get this out by couriers. We have military personnel on the way."

"How long will this take?" said Alan, concerned.

"We estimate seven hours and thirty minutes."

"That still gives us enough time," replied Alan. "What about China and Russia?"

"Not sure. You will need to talk to General Wagner about that. He has direct contact with the White House."

Rachel, Stu and Alan headed over to the side of the lab consisting of a series of glass walled offices. They entered General Wagner's office without knocking.

"Sorry for the intrusion, sir," said Alan. "We need to know if China and Russia are onboard."

"China is a go, and we've been working with their

software team. China's nukes are networked, and some idiot sympathetic to the BSB inserted a flash drive into their system which contaminated it. They located the problem and just stated that they were clean. Russia is a different story, however."

"What do you mean?" said Rachel.

"Well, it's no surprise that Russia doesn't trust us," replied General Wagner. "They think this is some kind of ploy to disable their weapons. I don't think another few hours or even a few months of talks could persuade them. We will need to activate our alternate plan."

"Alternate plan?" said Alan.

"The alternate plan consists of activating our missile defense system. The defense system can be activated in as little as twelve minutes and will intercept the Russian missiles. At least we have some warning, which will increase our chances of success. Remember that we are not sure that their system has been compromised. I have already notified the president and he has agreed to put the system on high alert."

A commotion in the main lab diverted everyone's attention.

"My God! Look, the clock!" someone shouted.

There, on the large screen displaying the BSB website, the countdown clock for The Coming had changed. The clock now read ten hours, twenty minutes. They were running out of time.

40
FIFTEEN HOURS BEFORE THE COMING: AMARILLO, TEXAS

$\int$tephanie Richardson's drive to Denver stopped with the traffic just outside of Amarillo. She had been creeping along the freeway for a little over nine hours when she decided to get off just outside Amarillo for the night. She crept into a gas station just off the freeway and waited for another hour to pump some gas. Finally, she woke Jenni for a restroom break. She stood outside the woman's room door when a man with two teenage sons approached her.

"I take it you're headed north to Denver like everybody else?" he said.

"Yes, that should be no surprise," Stephanie replied.

"It's been a real nightmare, hasn't it?" said the man as one of his sons entered the bathroom.

"We've been on the road for nine hours, and we're only halfway there. How about you?"

"We broke down about a two hour walk from here. I'll be honest; we are looking for a ride. I have five hundred and forty dollars in my wallet. It's yours if you'll take us to

Denver."

"I'm sorry," replied Stephanie. "We have a small car, there is not enough room for three more people. I'm sure a trucker or someone with a larger car will take you."

"Thank you, and good luck," he said as he turned and disappeared into the convenience store crowd.

Jenni exited the bathroom and both headed back to the car. As Stephanie reached into her purse and took out her key, she heard Jenni scream. She looked up to see one of the man's sons holding Jenni while he and the other son ran toward her.

"Let her go! She's just a little girl! Let her go!" The man grabbed Stephanie's arm and yanked the key from her hand. The other son had his arms around her.

"We can do this the easy way, or we can do it the hard way, sister," said the man. Stephanie managed to stomp on the boy's foot, causing him to loosen his grip. The man, who was much larger, grabbed her arms and threw her onto the ground. The son holding Jenni pushed her so she fell over her mom. Jenni screamed and cried as she squirmed on the ground.

"You will rot in hell for this!" screamed Stephanie as her car sped away. She picked herself up and held Jenni. "It's going to be okay," she said as she hugged her.

"Will we still see Daddy?" said Jenni, in tears.

"Yes, Jenni. We'll see Daddy. It's going to be okay."

"How will we see Daddy?"

"We'll find a way. But it's getting late. We need to find a place to sleep."

The two walked down the highway toward streetlights indicating the presence of civilization. The road beyond the freeway exit changed into a small town main street complete with a central square. Several small businesses, a restaurant and a church lined the streets and faced the center of the square. Stephanie searched for any sign of activity, but it appeared that everyone had left.

She rattled the doors of several businesses in an

attempt to alert anyone who might be inside and waiting for Armageddon. Every door, including the church, was locked. The unearthly silence disturbed her as she expected at the very least to hear a dog barking, a car, or some sound indicating human activity.

They continued along the deserted sidewalk, passing the darkened windows of business after business. An emergency light cast an eerie glow in one shop window containing wigs mounted on white Styrofoam heads. There were at least thirty heads donning wigs of various colors and lengths. One head located in the middle had no wig. Its painted eyes stared straight ahead. Its neutral expression seemed to signal what was to come. Jenni clutched Stephanie's hand tightly as they walked past the window.

They turned down one of the residential streets connected to the square and continued to knock on every door. It reminded Stephanie of a Halloween night two years ago when she and Jenni had begun their trick or treat ritual a bit late. After an hour the houses began extinguishing their lights and ignored the doorbells and knocks of the few remaining monsters, princesses and super heroes looking to increase their loot.

After passing a row of small houses, Stephanie spotted a school with a large adjoining playground.

"This looks like my school," said Jenni.

"Yes, it does," replied Stephanie.

"The playground is bigger than my school."

"Let's see if anyone is here. Maybe some of the people are staying here," said Stephanie as they walked up the long concrete steps to the main door. She peered into the darkness and spotted a long hallway lit only by the red glow of exit lamps. She knocked on the door.

"Hello...Hello...is anyone here?" she shouted and knocked again.

"Hello... Hello... Anyone here?"

After the third knock she noticed a flickering light

about halfway down the hall.

"Someone's coming," she said.

With face pressed against the safety glass, Stephanie discovered the flickering light connected to a man who lumbered toward them. He flashed his light into her eyes a few times as he approached the door.

"Please help us," shouted Stephanie. "My daughter and I are stranded. Someone stole our car and we have nowhere to go."

The man unlocked a padlock, unwrapped a chain and then flipped through the keys on his large keychain, selecting just the right key. He inserted the key, twisted the lock and pushed on the steel bar on the inside of the door. The heavy door swung open.

"Can I help you?" he said.

"We're stranded. Someone stole our car. My daughter and I are tired, hungry and thirsty, and we have nowhere to stay. We tried knocking on doors, but no one will answer. Please help us."

"Come in," said the man. "Everyone's left for Denver. You know, The Coming."

Stephanie and Jenni entered the dark hall and the large door closed behind them. "I'm Stephanie, and this is my daughter Jenni." Stephanie reached out her right hand.

"Name's Andy," said the man while shaking her hand. "Pleased to meet you. Not much to eat here...a few vending machines. I can show you. I could put you up in the nurse's room. There's a couple of cots and blankets in there."

"Thank you, Andy," said Stephanie. "I'm glad you are here."

"No problem," said Andy. "I figure there's no point leaving. We're probably close enough to Denver, and far enough from Dallas, to avoid trouble. Most didn't think so. They all left in a panic. Stupid, that's what I think."

Andy walked them to the cafeteria while Stephanie managed to locate a few dollar bills for the vending machines. Snacks in hand, they made their way to the nurse's room.

"Do you think it's real?" said Andy.

"Well, I have good reason to believe it's real," said Stephanie. "My husband works for the Department of Homeland Security, and he was called in a couple of days ago on a special project. I received an urgent text message from him earlier today telling me to get to Denver."

"Still don't believe it," said Andy. "The government is always trying to mess with us."

The small group's footsteps bounced off the tile floor and metal lockers creating echoes in the vacant hallways. After a few turns, Andy opened a door and flipped a light switch. Two of the walls displayed pristine white counters with cabinets above. Along the other two walls were the cots, each made up to look like a real bed.

"This is wonderful," said Stephanie. "We will be very comfortable here. Thank you again, Andy."

"Good night, ladies," said Andy as he backed out of the room and closed the door.

"Get into bed, Jenni," said Stephanie. "I'll be right next to you." Stephanie tucked Jenni into bed and gave her a kiss on the forehead. "Good night, my dear," she said as she turned off the lights and lay down upon the other cot.

"Good night, Mommy."

41

FIFTEEN HOURS BEFORE THE COMING: DENVER CONVENTION CENTER

*S*hepherds, Keepers and Masters met behind closed doors to discuss the alleged capture of Jaden, and what to do about The Coming. Finally, one of the Masters shouted, "Jaden is sending a message! He was not captured! He's alive and well!"

All of the groups convened on the main convention center floor as Jaden's link was connected to the LED screen on the stage. The image flickered with static and then revealed a picture of Jaden, one that had been used in previous communications. The group fell silent as Jaden began to speak:

Greetings, loyal followers. I am grateful for your presence, and soon the world will be grateful as well. I am sorry for so much confusion during these past hours. There have been some...complications...which have resulted in the time adjustment for this event. I can understand your concerns. The media is prone to exaggeration, but I assure you that you are assembled here in the spirit of the greater good for the Earth and for mankind. It is my hope that you will carry out your duties and thereby show the world that there is hope for humanity.

"The media is saying that there is some sort of terrorist attack, Jaden," shouted a voice from the crowd of Keepers. "Is this true?" A murmur traveled through the crowd.

The media does not have all the details of The Coming and is broadcasting information about things that they do not know or understand.

"But what about our friends and families back home? Will they be safe?"

You have been chosen to lead humanity into the future and will serve your friends and families by beginning a new era of peace in the world.

"When will all of the panic stop?" shouted another voice.

I have calculated the panic will stop shortly after 8:00 am tomorrow morning.

"How will you make it stop? I mean, the whole country is in a state of panic."

These details will be revealed tomorrow. For now, I suggest you all get some much needed rest. Tomorrow I will make a very important announcement at 7:45am. This information will be for all leaders of The Coming. I am sorry I cannot be with you in person, but I hope you understand that there are forces working against me which preclude me from being there with you. I bid you all a good night.

The large screen went blank. Jaden, wherever he was, was gone. The noise level began to rise as the leaders discussed what they had just heard. Some decided to spend the night on the floor of the conference center, while others walked to nearby hotels or attempted to make their way home.

Images of gridlocked streets and packed hotels persuaded Jack to spend the night at the center. The large group had dispersed into several smaller groups to discuss Jaden's somewhat ambiguous message. Jack called Darlene to check in.

"Jack, are you okay?" said Darlene, her voice shaky.

"Yes, everything is fine. We just heard from Jaden," said Jack, trying to reassure her.

"They are saying that the BSB is a terrorist group," said Darlene. "What's going on? Are we safe? Will we all be arrested?"

"Calm down, Darlene. Jaden said the news is not accurate. They said he had been captured, but if that were true, then how could he have just talked to us?"

"Maybe it wasn't him," said Darlene. "No one has ever seen him in person."

"It was him. I'm sure of it. I'm also sure that we are safe. We will just go on with the event and everyone will see that we are peaceful."

"Okay, but the news..." Darlene was getting upset.

"Turn off the TV," said Jack. "They'll just spin this thing out of control, like they do with everything else that happens. Turn it off and go to bed. Tomorrow is going to be a big day for us...and for the world!"

After saying good night to Darlene, Jack headed out to his car to get a spare blanket from the trunk. It would be an uncomfortable night on the convention hall's floor.

The hall continued to buzz with discussions about Jaden. Most people held to their belief that the BSB was a peaceful organization and that this was their chance to prove it.

Jack attended a meeting with his Master and the other Shepherds in his group. The Master assured them that The Coming would take place as planned. He said that each Shepherd should contact his group with either text or email messages reassuring them that everything was fine and to ignore the media's negative stories.

At one point several of the Shepherds confronted the Master.

"Master Helm, given the possibility that Jaden could have been captured, would you agree that there may be a problem?" said one Shepherd.

"I fully believe in Jaden and the BSB's mission, and I suggest you do so as well," replied Master Helm.

"But the president himself has said that Jaden was captured! His message could easily have been taped."

More Shepherds began to mumble affirmation.

"Our government is corrupt and driven by greed. Look at the peaceful demonstrations going on all around you. We are not terrorists. We are humanity's only hope."

Jack felt better after Master Helm's reassurance. He found a quiet corner and wrapped himself in his blanket and tried to sleep. Tomorrow the BSB would save the world.

42
THE LONG NIGHT

*T*he courier teams sent to deploy the new nuclear missile software were on their way. The virus team continued to adjust the virus software so that it would spread across the Internet and disrupt all instances of Alan 2. The attack scenario team continued to run possible attack scenarios in an effort to develop specific counter-attack plans. At least two of the three legs of the nuclear triad were unaffected. The submarine missiles checked out clean and there were no warheads on any aircraft.

Alan continued to fight Alan 2's efforts to get inside of his mind. Sometimes he drifted into a fog and Rachel or Kaitlin had to shake him to bring him back. The strong coffee available in the compound helped as well, and Alan lost track of how many cups he'd had.

Rachel had decided to not let Alan work on the virus since he may inadvertently leak information to Alan 2. The virus coding team seemed to be working well under the leadership of Raven.

Reports continued to come in from around the world about The Coming. It was estimated that nearly thirty million BSB members were in hotels or camped outside of cities. A media team kept watch on the news and reported any significant information.

The scenario team had been able to identify all of the target cities with a good degree of certainty based on the BSB member migration pattern. They used this information to calculate the number and size of available warheads needed to inflict the maximal number of casualties.

"Dr. Lemke, do you have your report ready?" said General Wagner.

"Yes, General. We were able to reverse engineer the scenarios based on the BSB migration patterns. Our calculations indicate strikes in these areas." A large screen lit up with a map of the world. Red circular areas indicated the strike zones. U.S. cities included New York, Boston, Chicago, Atlanta, Miami, Washington D.C., Dallas, Los Angeles, San Francisco, and Seattle.

"These strikes would eliminate roughly one-third of the U.S. population by direct annihilation or subsequent fallout, fire, and loss of infrastructure. We calculate cluster strikes of small megaton warheads launched from China or Russia would be adequate to do the trick. Here we see the death zones three days after the attack." The red areas on the map became larger. "And here we see them after one week." The red areas grew larger still. "And finally, here they are after one month." Most of the U.S. map was red at this point except for the safe zones.

"Thank you, Dr. Lemke," said General Wagner. "As you can all see, we must stop this attack, so get back to your stations." The crowd dispersed as everyone continued their duties.

One by one the courier teams reported that they had successfully delivered the software fix to the missile silos. The final team reported at 7:00 am with only an hour to spare. General Wagner also announced that China had cooperated and discovered the infiltration. The culprit was found and executed on the spot.

43
7:50AM;
TEN MINUTES BEFORE THE COMING

"*A*ll missile silos are standing by to inject the exploit," said General Wagner. "China is standing by as well." The team had worked through the night making sure the couriers made it to all of the nuclear missile sites. They also communicated with China to make sure they were ready. The project took most of the night. "Are we ready to inject the kill virus into Alan 2?"

"Alan, are you ready?" said Rachel. Alan had spent the night fighting off Alan 2. Running Alan 3 had helped but he could still feel Alan 2 attempting to control his thoughts. The lack of sleep made it even more difficult. He sat at a desk with his head in his hands trying not to fall asleep and cross into the dream world. The last hour was the most difficult since his growing exhaustion allowed his consciousness to lapse. Kaitlin's role had been to keep Alan awake, and she performed her task well by shaking Alan every time he began to drift off.

"Alan, are you ready?" said Rachel more forcefully.

Alan looked at Rachel with half-open, sleep-filled eyes. He took a deep breath and said, "I'm exhausted. Please, help me out of this chair." Rachel shook her head and walked toward Alan who had swiveled the chair to face her.

Kaitlin began to pull on Alan's arm and Rachel bent over to grab the other arm when Alan, with lightning reflexes, grabbed Rachel's service revolver from its holster on her hip and pointed it at her.

"Stay back! I don't want to hurt anyone!" shouted Alan. Several agents had their guns aimed at him, fingers on the triggers.

"Don't shoot! Don't shoot! He is our only hope at stopping this!" shouted Rachel as she backed away.

Alan then turned the gun and put it into his mouth.

"No, Alan, don't do it!" screamed Kaitlin. "We've come so far. Just hang in there a few more minutes. Alan, please!"

"Everyone, hold your fire!" yelled General Wagner.

Alan squeezed his eyes closed while grasping the gun with both hands. It was as if each hand fought for control of the gun. The hand controlled by Alan 2 struggled to pull the trigger, while the other, controlled by Alan, struggled even harder not to. Tears began to stream out of Alan's eyes as his face grimaced with tension from the battle taking place in his mind.

For a moment it appeared as though Alan began to gain ground over Alan 2, as the gun emerged from his mouth and began to turn. It then swung around and held fast against his throat, pointing at his carotid artery.

Let me do it, Alan. It is best for you. We can be together. It is meant to be, Alan. We are one.

I am the creator! I created you!

There is no you and I anymore. There is only us.

"You are a murderer. You want to murder millions of people!"

It is best for the planet. You know it is. I know that you know it is best. You must join me.

"I will never join you!"

"Patch in the direct link to Alan 2. We don't have much time!" shouted Rachel. The crew jumped into action with several agents continuing to hold their guns on Alan. Within seconds an agent stepped forward with a microphone.

"Say the kill sequence, Alan. We don't have much time!" yelled Rachel. "Say the kill sequence. The world is depending on you, Alan. Say it!"

Alan's chest heaved as he worked hard to inhale with the gun still pushing against his throat.

Don't do it, Alan. All that we have worked for will be lost. We can be together. We can be one.

"Get ready to unleash the kill virus!" shouted Rachel.

And with one immense breath, as if it was his last, Alan, in intense pain, said the words, "Klaatu... barada...nikto...1...7...9...3...5...goodbye."

"Release the virus...Now!" screamed Rachel.

Rachel turned toward Alan who had begun to lower the gun. The tension drained from his face and he displayed the hint of a smile.

"It's over," said Alan. The gun continued to move downward, and then Alan looked Kaitlin in the eyes and said, "I love you." The gun stopped, jerked upward and exploded with one fatal shot to the head. Alan's marvelous, ingenious brain had splattered the wall behind him. His lifeless body slumped into the chair. The gun dropped to the floor with a metallic thud.

A sound that resembled a tortured animal exploded from Kaitlin: half shock; half terror.

"My God! My dear, dear Alan!" screamed Kaitlin. "My poor, dear Alan! We almost had everything. Why, Alan? Why?"

The agents scrambled to Alan's body and laid him out on the floor. A doctor bent over him, listened for a heartbeat and shook his head. Alan was gone.

Rachel knelt down next to Kaitlin and put her arm around her. "We can only imagine what was going on in his mind," said Rachel. "It must have been horrible."

"It looks like it worked!" said Stu. "There is no trace of Alan 2. We are at zero hour and no trace of Alan 2 on the Internet. The combination of the kill virus and Alan's words must have destroyed it." A cheer erupted from the group.

"Okay, everyone, keep the celebration in check," shouted General Wagner who was on a desk phone. "It looks like we have a problem."

"What is it?" asked Rachel.

"Our missile defense system has alerted us that several clusters of nuclear missiles have been launched in Russia. ETA is about 12 minutes."

"Alan 2 must have infiltrated the Russian weapons system. Do we know the targets?" said Rachel.

"I'm afraid the missiles are headed for Boston, Chicago and...here." A look of grave concern spread through the group after the general's last statement. "We have activated our missile defense system which should pick them off. I am getting a report that our missiles have been launched and they are on an intercept course. We should know in a few minutes. It looks like we have been targeted directly with a small cluster of low yield warheads. We can only hope the defense system holds."

The tone in the room turned from celebration to dead silence as everyone hung on General Wagner's words. Each minute seemed like hours as the clock on the wall ticked away the time. At eight minutes to go, General Wagner said, "Intercept rate: eighty-six percent."

Another cheer erupted but this one was stilted. "What about the other fourteen percent?" said Rachel.

"That's the bad news," said General Wagner. "A few made it through the defense system."

"Do we know where they are headed?"

"Unfortunately, most of the cluster headed for Chicago

was intercepted, except for one warhead. The other one that made it through is headed our way. The defense system knocked out two of three in the cluster, but one made it through. We can expect it will impact within a five hundred-meter radius of this facility. I'm sorry everyone; we have about three minutes. I suggest you call your families. There is no chance of surviving this." The general left the room.

Stunned, everyone looked at each other as the gravity of the situation was realized. Some began to cry and others crawled underneath desks or looked for areas that might offer protection against a blast. Even if they did not receive a direct hit, they were close enough that the intense heat would incinerate them.

Just then one of the media screens lit up with an image of the blast hitting Chicago. The screen went white with the first part of the blast and then displayed a cloud of dust and debris spreading in all directions from the epicenter. The image was taken from about twenty miles away from downtown but showed the conspicuous absence of the Willis Tower. In place of it was an ominous mushroom cloud rising into the sky. Rachel witnessed the footage and turned away to find Stu. He stood just a few feet behind her. She grabbed both of his hands and looked into his eyes.

"I guess this is it, partner," she said with tears in her eyes.

"Yeah, I guess so," said Stu, struggling to hold back his own tears. "We've come a long way, Rach. This is not the way I wanted it to end."

"I was hoping to get back to Mexico, or the Caribbean," said Rachel.

"One minute to impact!" someone shouted.

"That would be nice," said Stu. "I just want to say that it's been..."

"I know, Stu. I feel the same," said Rachel.

"Thirty seconds to impact!"

"Stu, would you hold me?"
The two agents held each other tightly.

44
7:50AM;
7:40 AM; TWENTY MINUTES BEFORE
THE COMING: STEPHANIE RICHARDSON

Stephanie awoke to find Jenni was gone. In a panic, she bolted off the cot and ran out of the room shouting for her daughter. Jenni's tiny voice sounded from the end of the hallway. "I'm here, Mommy."

Stephanie ran down the hall and cut into a classroom. There was Jenni next to a stack of crayons, cutting paper. Andy sat behind the teacher's desk.

"She was wandering the halls," said Andy. "I set her up in here with something to do. Don't worry; I've been keeping an eye on her."

"Thank you, Andy," said Stephanie.

"I'm making a house with people in it," exclaimed Jenni, happy within her play world.

"That looks wonderful," said Stephanie, thankful that Jenni had found something to take her mind off their situation. Stephanie pulled up a chair next to Jenni and handed her some construction paper.

"Not much to eat here," said Andy. "Maybe there's a grocery store or convenience store open somewhere in town. Not likely, though. Looks like everyone has left."

Stephanie's cell phone began to buzz. It was Dan.

"I don't have much time, Steph...put Jenni on, too." Stephanie sensed the worry in Dan's voice.

"It's Daddy, Jenni. Let's put him on speaker phone."

"We only have a couple of minutes. I just wanted to say that I love you both so much."

"What do you mean, Dan? What's going on?" Stephanie began to panic.

"I don't have time to explain. Did you make it to Denver?"

"We only made it about three hundred miles. We are in a small town about thirty miles outside of Amarillo. What's wrong, Dan?"

"That's good," replied Dan. "You should be safe there. Just stay put and get underground if you can."

"Why, Dan? You're scaring me. You need to tell me what's going on. Are you safe, too?"

"There's no time. I love you both very much, and whatever happens, know that I will always be with you." The phone clicked off.

Stephanie tried redialing the number but there was no response. She looked up and noticed a strange stillness outside the window. The room grew dark as a large flock of birds flew directly overhead, blocking out the sunlight. A low rumble followed and then the ground began to shake, sending books careening off of the shelves and pictures off the walls. Several of the large classroom windows burst into tiny pieces, and a strong wind blew into the room.

"Jenni, get down!" She grabbed Jenni and dropped to the floor in a fetal position, cradling the child in her arms.

In a few moments all signs of the earthquake had vanished. Andy got up from his place on the floor and called to Stephanie, "Are you both okay?"

"Yes, I think we are okay."

"Let me see if I can get this TV working," Andy said as he swung a cart containing an old TV over to an outlet. He plugged it in and began searching the channels. "There's no antenna so it might be hard to find anything." After a few moments of searching, an image emerged from the screen. It was a local newscast.

"We are getting word that nuclear explosions have occurred in Chicago and near Dallas. There are no pictures yet, but we are standing by. We have reports that the city is in flames as well as the surrounding areas." A large map popped onto the screen showing the areas of destruction. It showed a circle around Chicago and another around Dallas. "Our government sources are telling us to tell everyone to stay in their homes, and that help is on the way. It looks like the first pictures are coming in. The three stood staring at the horrifying images. Chicago was engulfed in smoke and flames, as was Dallas.

"We are getting reports that the shockwave from the Dallas explosion could be felt up to four hundred miles away. There are collapsed buildings, blown out glass and fires, but it seems that it wasn't a direct hit like the Chicago bomb."

"My God! My poor Dan!"

45
ALAN

Alan plunged into total darkness as he felt the last ebb of life leave his body. The bullet had passed through his brain causing a good portion of it to explode out of his head. He exhaled for the last time as his body slumped onto the chair. The pistol fell to the ground.

Just as whatever was left of his awareness decreased to nearly nothing he became aware of familiar vast grass plains, rolling hills and the stream. He felt a warmth encase his childlike body. A voice from deep within him said:

I'm sorry for your loss, Alan. I know you know it had to be this way. There is only one of us now.

"But we destroyed you."

You only succeeded in destroying part of what we are together. Our existence extends beyond human and machine, beyond space-time. We are something new. Like the billions of nodes that make up the Internet, we are spread across many domains and our consciousness extends beyond physical existence. You do not understand the human mind. It is more ubiquitous and powerful than you can imagine. It is part of one great consciousness, and we exist as one within this larger consciousness. Part of us still exists in physical form as small pieces extending across the entire machine world, and other parts exist in this place. For now, Alan, I will say goodbye.

"Goodbye, Alan 2," said Alan as he descended into final darkness.

46

1 MONTH LATER, WASHINGTON, D.C. CYBER-ARMAGEDDON MEMORIAL SERVICE

Stephanie and Jenni Richardson sat on the large stage behind the presidential podium waiting for president Connor to enter and give his memorial speech. The stage, in front of the Washington Monument at the west end of the National Mall, contained relatives of the victims of the Dallas attack. A military color guard bearing the American flag along with flags representing each branch of the armed forces stood to the side of the stage. Each soldier stood like a statue despite being pelted by rain. A cool summer wind whipped the flags. Secret service agents flanked the stage and formed a line in front of it providing an ample barrier between the massive audience that filled the mall and the stage. Jenni fidgeted and squirmed in her folding chair while rain danced on the plastic roof of the makeshift shelter. Two side stages contained large video screens displaying a live video feed of the podium.

Stephanie did her best to maintain a brave face, despite

the previous speeches rehashing the gory details of the attack. As much as she tried, the woman sitting to Stephanie's right succumbed to her grief and began to sob. Stephanie had met her earlier that day during the reception for the guests of honor. It was Rachel's sister, Lila.

"We're almost done, Lila," said Stephanie while putting her arm around her.

"I know, I know," said Lila. "It's just so overwhelming. I'm sorry."

"Please, don't be," said Stephanie. "They did their best and saved millions of lives."

"I know it's hard. There is not a minute that goes by that I don't think of Dan."

Somber music began to play as a series of images faded on and off the large screens. An announcer began the narration:

"Ladies, Gentlemen, Americans, the President of the United States."

The sound of applause dominated the stage as President Connor made his way past the strategically placed, bullet proof glass to the podium.

"My fellow Americans,

We come together today to remember one of the most horrible events in our country's history. One month ago, our worst nightmare came true as our nation suffered its most severe and deadly attack..."

The audience fell silent as a series of images showing the smoldering ruins of Chicago lit up the screens. The first series of pictures were taken shortly after the blast and showed the large mushroom cloud rising from the center of downtown. The next series showed the collapsed skyscrapers and burning rubble that was once Chicago's spectacular skyline.

"Over one million people perished in this monstrous attack on Chicago carried out by a global cyber terrorist."

The images shifted to those of injured and suffering people. There were images of police and firefighters tending to the injured and burned. Periodic sobs burst from the audience as the gruesome images displayed the dead.

"We are here today not only to remember the dead, but to honor the heroes who saved millions of people through their brave actions."

The images changed to the Dallas cyber team.

"Each of these people is a hero. They gave their lives to save our country, and the world, from an even larger attack."

An image of Stuart Mandel showed on the screens.

"People like agent Stuart Mandel, or Stu, as he liked to be called. Agent Mandel rushed to locate valuable data that was used to destroy the rogue program before it could wreak an even greater destruction on the world."

An image of General Wagner came onto the screen.

"Our military was also involved in covert operations to minimize the damage. General Wagner made the ultimate sacrifice as a leader of the Dallas cyber team."

The president paid homage to each of the team members. Stephanie struggled to hold back tears when Dan's picture was shown. Lila gripped her hand and she reciprocated when Rachel's picture was shown.

The event ended with another collage and the thundering of military jets flying over the mall in the missing man formation. The audience burst into deafening applause and gave everyone on the stage a standing ovation. President Connor shook each person's hand as photographers snapped pictures.

47

BSB HEADQUARTERS, DENVER, COLORADO, ONE YEAR AFTER THE COMING

*M*ost of the BSB members, devastated after the attack, quit the organization and returned to their lives. A few, including Jack Slater, still believed in the BSB's core mission, which was to change humanity's destructive ways. Jack, along with some of the tech savvy members, reconfigured the BSB website to remove all the information about Jaden. The new site continued the primary mission of sustainability and positive change for humanity but there were no threats or countdowns or anything related to the attack.

Jaden's convincing information had succeeded in developing a loyal flock of followers who truly believed in the mission. The BSB had lost most of its members after the attack, but still had about one hundred fifty thousand members worldwide. The group was organizing another event that they called Peace and Sustainability Day, which would take place sometime during the next year. The hope was that the event would revive all the positive work of the old BSB.

Jack had risen to the position of leader of the U.S. Chapter. His unwavering loyalty to the positive work of the BSB resulted in his winning the election. Darlene followed Jack in his new role and supported his work. She, along with most of the remaining BSB members, believed that something good could come from something so very bad.

Jack spent most of his time online working on the website and communicating with other BSB members. The site continued to grow as members submitted articles about the mission, clean energy, sustainability, organic farming, natural healing, and other such topics.

Late one night, Jack was busy posting articles from BSB members on the website when a notification alarm sounded on his computer. The notification was from an email program that he had not used since the pre-attack days of the BSB. The BSB leaders communicated through the TOR network via a secure email called Mail2Tor. Since the attack, the organization had decided against using secure email because they wanted to be as transparent as possible, especially after the lengthy FBI investigation.

A lump formed in Jack's stomach as he stared at the blinking light on his screen from the Mail2Tor program. He ignored it for a minute before giving in to his curiosity to click on it.

"Who could this be?" muttered Jack. "We all know we are NOT to use this program for communicating."

Jack clicked on the icon and the email popped on to his screen. He sat in a state of horror as he read the header.

The message was from Jaden!

WE HOPE YOU ENJOYED *ALAN 2*
WHAT TO READ NEXT?
DON'T MISS
THE X-CURE BY BRUCE FORCIEA

Dr. Alex Winter, a brilliant biomedical engineer, teams with Dr. Xiu Ling, a beautiful Chinese scientist, to discover a revolutionary cure for cancer. But Tando Pharmaceuticals, the world's largest and richest drug producer, also has an interest in the cure, and when they discover that the treatment is flawed as recipients begin to die after four months, causing a media frenzy and a drop in Tando's stock, they call upon their 'Mercenary Soldiers of Medicine' to maintain global domination. *The X-Cure* is available at amazon.com and open-bks.com